Grace rolled her eyes. "Is there anything you enjoy?"

He enjoyed verbally sparring with her. Making that blush rise up from her ample chest, over her neck and onto her cheeks. If she was beautiful ordinarily, it was nothing compared to when she was angry. Her green eyes sparkled even more.

Eyes sparkling? What the hell was he thinking? He shook his head and swept his arm for her to walk past him.

"I enjoy a great many things, Grace Harris. Maybe one day you'll find out all about me."

She stepped closer to him. So close that her scent made its way to his nose. He didn't know if it was her shampoo or perfume or lotion. Not that it mattered one bit. Grace smelled absolutely delectable.

"Oh, I think I know plenty about you now, Xander Ryan."

He didn't back down. He leaned into her. "Astound me."

"You're cocky and way too self-assured," she said. "You don't like weddings and think wedding planners are silly." She took a breath. "If you weren't Jack's best friend and he didn't vouch for you, I wouldn't even waste my precious time talking to you now."

He pinned her with his best seductive stare and lowered his voice. "But you are talking to me now."

She gulped. "Not for long."

**SOMETHING TRUE:**
**Because the perfect fit is hard to find.**

Dear Reader,

I've always loved "opposites attract" stories, which is why I'm so excited about this next book in my Something True series. You met Grace and Xander in *The Dating Arrangement*. But they didn't exactly get off to the best of starts...

See, Grace is a wedding planner who is absolutely in love with love. She's optimistic, hopeful, and always sees the good in life. Xander, on the other hand, is a divorce attorney who plans to avoid marriage like the plague. He's a cynic, for sure. The only thing they seem to have in common is an intense attraction to each other.

So, what's going to happen when they have to come together to plan their best friends' wedding in only three short weeks? Will they fight all the way to the altar? Or will they be able to make some kind of truce? Better question: Will that truce extend beyond the wedding? You'll have to read to find out!

I hope you enjoy *The Wedding Truce*! I love to connect with readers, so please visit my website and subscribe to my newsletter at kerricarpenter.com, or find me on Facebook, Twitter and Instagram as AuthorKerri.

Happy reading and glitter toss,

*Kerri Carpenter*

# The Wedding Truce

*Kerri Carpenter*

**HARLEQUIN** SPECIAL EDITION

Recycling programs
for this product may
not exist in your area.

ISBN-13: 978-1-335-89433-5

The Wedding Truce

**Printed in U.S.A.**

Award-winning romance author **Kerri Carpenter** writes contemporary romances that are sweet, sexy and sparkly. When she's not writing, Kerri enjoys reading, cooking, watching movies, taking Zumba classes, rooting for Pittsburgh sports teams and anything sparkly. Kerri lives in northern Virginia with her adorable (and mischievous) rescued poodle mix, Harry. Visit Kerri at her website, kerricarpenter.com, on Facebook (Facebook.com/authorkerri), Twitter and Instagram (@authorkerri), or subscribe to her newsletter.

### Books by Kerri Carpenter

### Harlequin Special Edition

### *Something True*

*The Dating Arrangement*

### *Saved by the Blog*

*Falling for the Right Brother*
*Bidding on the Bachelor*
*Bayside's Most Unexpected Bride*

Visit the Author Profile page
at Harlequin.com for more titles.

For Carlene, my dear friend and fellow Mermaid.
Thank you for always being there for me and for
bringing your sunny San Diego sparkles into my life.
That's why you're MY hero!

# Chapter One

"I love you, Grace Harris."

Grace grinned at the words she'd wanted to hear her entire life. Of course, she'd been waiting for a devastatingly handsome and charming prince to utter them. Instead, she was hearing them from Katie Mason, a client engaged to her own Prince Charming.

"I'm serious, I could kiss you."

Grace laughed. "I'm not sure how George would feel about that."

Katie shook her head. "I don't think he would care one bit when he learns you've figured out how to finally make this wedding come together. I never thought our styles would mesh, but you came up with the perfect plan."

Blending family traditions at a wedding wasn't a novelty—though it wasn't always easy. Grace had worked on hundreds of weddings and there was often some negotiating involved, but everything was always resolved in time to give the bride and groom their perfect day.

She rose from her desk. "It's all in a day's work, Katie. I'm just happy that you're happy. The ceremony is going to be beautiful, and the reception will be extraordinary."

Katie stood as well and scooted around the antique desk to give Grace a quick hug. "And thanks for staying late to help me work all of this out. I know our appointment was supposed to end forty-five minutes ago. You're the best wedding planner ever."

"What a great testimonial to add to my website," Grace said with a wink.

They began walking toward the door, a subtle move Grace hoped wouldn't suggest she was running late due to Katie's earlier meltdown about the logistics of her wedding. She had a date to get ready for, but at the same time, her business was important to her.

"Don't worry. I'll be giving you testimonials, bouquets of flowers, my undying love..."

"All of which are unnecessary. I just want to make your special day amazing."

"I've already recommended you to two of my friends. They're both newly engaged."

Grace stifled the happy dance Katie's words incited. She'd started her wedding-planning business less than two years ago. Only recently had she begun to see a steady profit, so word of mouth between brides was definitely a boost she could use.

The two women said goodbye, and Grace hurried back to her office to tidy up the space before calling it a day. She paused as she picked up a bridal magazine. The issue boasted Florida weddings, and the cover showed a bride wearing the most gorgeous princess ball gown at one of the Disney parks in Orlando.

Two of Grace's favorite things on the planet: wedding dresses and the town where she grew up. Of course, she also loved everything about weddings, too, but she'd always believed that a great wedding began with the gown. That's why she'd loved working at Kleinfeld Bridal in New York City one summer during college. She'd been a lowly intern dashing off on coffee runs, but at least she got to be surrounded by exquisite dresses every day.

She took another look at the bridal magazine, paying close attention to the gown. One of her current clients was a traditional bride throwing a black-tie wedding. She would absolutely love this ball gown.

She ran her hand over the glossy publication and allowed herself a moment to dream about her own wedding. Her own happy ending. Her own Prince Charming.

Grace had wanted to be a wedding planner ever since she planned her first Barbie wedding when she was a little girl. Setting up her dolls' special day had been a great way to drown out the real world. While she prepared her dolls to say their "I do's" in the corner of her cramped bedroom, she didn't have to think about her irresponsible mother, their cold trailer, or the unpredictable and scary life they lived.

When yet another of her mother's new boyfriends came by, she could escape into the happy world where people fell in love and got married. Even if her mother didn't follow that path, Grace knew she would no doubt get the same happy ending as her dolls.

She had to.

And everything would be perfect.

Luckily, later in life, she'd been accepted into Disney's internship program, where she'd been able to learn how to plan their famous nuptials with real live people instead of plastic dolls.

Grace shook her head, her long hair falling over her shoulder. She needed to stop daydreaming, so she threw down the magazine and quickly finished cleaning up the space. With a final glance to check that everything was in place, she shut down her laptop, locked her drawers and turned off the lights.

Then she closed the French doors that led to her office and walked up the stairs to the second floor of the town house she shared with her best friend, Emerson. The first floor of the traditional row home had been converted to offices for both herself and Emerson. The second floor was their living room, dining area and kitchen, and both of their bedrooms and bathrooms were on the third floor.

Not only was it the best commute ever, but Grace also loved living right in the center of Old Town, the historic and trendy area of Alexandria that welcomed tourists, families and locals. She loved the energy of the area with its cobblestone streets, plethora of bars, restaurants and shops, and proximity to the Potomac River and Washington, DC.

Of course, she was also thrilled she got to live with her best friend. Emerson first suggested the arrangement after Emerson's fiancé had broken up with her—and left her with a huge mortgage to pay.

Grace shuddered as she remembered the pain her best friend had endured at the betrayal.

The silver lining—and Grace always looked for the silver lining—was that the two of them got to live together. And the home office space was a perk they both loved.

Grace entered her bedroom and threw her bag onto the frilly eyelet bedspread. She immediately stalked to her closet, rifled through the hangers and grabbed a dress. Then she crossed to her dressing table and began fixing up her makeup. She didn't have much time to get ready for her date.

She didn't have much enthusiasm, either. Which seemed to be a habit with her lately.

Grace Harris was in love with love. Well. The *idea* of love. She'd yet to experience it for herself, after all. In her line of work, though, she got to help others achieve that dream— which only made her long for it even more… The anticipation of a crush. The rush of first love. The enduring comfort of long-term love.

Or, what she assumed would be an enduring comfort.

"You'll get there," she said to her reflection.

Yet, as she ran a brush through her long, black hair and applied her favorite matte red lipstick, there was a niggling thought in the back of her mind. Something that was warning her that she wasn't quite as excited about her date tonight as she should be.

A sigh escaped her painted lips. This would be her fourth date with Derek and if she was being honest with herself, she'd had to talk herself into seeing him again. Which didn't make sense.

Derek Whittaker was successful, handsome and driven. Any woman would kill to go out with him.

She changed into her dress and shoes.

He was also a bit egotistical, kind of full of himself and sort of a bore, too.

She did a little turn in front of her full-length mirror. Her nose crinkled as she took in her shoes. They weren't right.

"Definitely the strappy ones," Emerson said from the doorway.

Grace nearly jumped out of her skin. "Oh, my god, you scared me! I didn't know you were back from that meeting yet." She took a minute to catch her breath. "Which strappy ones? It's not like I only have one pair," she said, laughing.

Completely at home amid her friend's things—which made sense, since they constantly perused each other's wardrobes—Emerson walked to the closet, rummaged around and produced a pair of nude heels. Grace put them on, then did another spin for her best friend.

Emerson whistled. "Grace, you look gorgeous." She tilted her head. "Does Derek deserve this?"

"I'm not dressing for Derek. I dress for one person only and that's myself. If he enjoys it, too, well, that's a bonus."

Emerson flopped down on Grace's bed. "To be honest, I'm surprised you're going out with him again."

"You know my rule." Grace added her favorite pair of silver heart earrings.

"I know, I know. You have to give every guy three chances. But if I remember correctly, you're past three dates."

Grace held up four fingers. She faced Emerson and frowned. "To be perfectly honest, I didn't really want to go out again. But he has this work thing and practically begged me to accompany him." She shrugged one shoulder. "I felt bad not giving it one more chance, so I said yes."

"Of course you did." Emerson rolled her eyes dramatically. "You are too nice, Grace Harris."

"As all wannabe princesses should be."

"Forget about Derek. We have more important things to discuss."

"We do?" Grace spritzed herself with her favorite perfume.

"Yes. You may not be aware, but I am getting married," Emerson announced.

"What?" Grace played along. "You're engaged? When did that happen?"

Of course, Grace was aware of her best friend's recent engagement to Jack Wright. The two of them were beyond perfect for each other. She'd seen the sparks flying from the first time she'd witnessed them together.

Emerson threw one of the twenty throw pillows from Grace's bed at her.

"Don't make me mad at you or I won't ask you to be my maid of honor."

"Em, are you serious? Me?"

"Of course, you." Emerson rose and crossed to Grace. "What do you say? Will you do it?"

"OMG, Em. Yes! I will!"

Emerson's eyes were shining with happiness. "I mean, I'm going to boss you around and claim it's 'my day' and all the usual crap brides say."

"I think I can handle it," she said, rolling her eyes and grinning.

"Will you be able to handle planning the wedding and being in it?" Emerson asked with concern.

Grace nodded emphatically. "Oh, hells yes. I've actually carved out some time around your big day so you will be getting all my personal attention as your wedding planner. And now your maid of honor." She squealed.

Suddenly, her gaze fell on a framed picture that had been taken of her, Emerson and Emerson's sister, Amelia, sitting on the dresser. She picked it up and handed it to her friend. "What about Amelia? I don't want to upset her. Shouldn't *she* be your matron of honor, or, um, I mean your maid of honor."

Amelia had just ended her own marriage after only six months. And from what Grace had heard, she wasn't having an easy time.

Emerson looked at the photo for a moment before returning it to the dresser. "You're going to be co-maids of honor. The only thing is, Amelia isn't in a great place, and I don't want to put her under a lot of pressure. So if it's okay, I'm going to rely on you for most of the traditional maid-of-honor duties."

"No problem. I completely understand." Grace glanced once more at the picture of Amelia. "Poor thing. How's she doing?"

"She's getting by. I know she's making the right decision, and I think she's going to be fine. Amelia's tougher than she realizes."

That was a relief to hear. Grace had known Emerson for years now and she was close with the entire Dewitt family.

As Grace put the finishing touches on her outfit, they continued talking about the wedding. It was interesting to watch her best friend, the calm and cool event planner, become frustrated over the details of her own wedding.

"What are you so worried about?" She grabbed Emerson's shoulders. "Everything is going to be fine. It'll be perfect. You'll see."

Emerson rolled her eyes. "You, my friend, are far too optimistic."

"Hey, that's supposed to be a good quality."

Grace's cell phone went off, and she saw a text message from Derek. He was outside. She could feel her smile fading. "Derek's here."

"Just remember that everything is going to be fine. No, perfect," Emerson said with fake enthusiasm, as she flung Grace's words back at her.

"Gee, thanks." Sometimes being optimistic took a lot of effort.

It took thirty minutes to get to the party in traffic and find street parking in congested Old Town.

"We really should have walked or taken an Uber," Grace said as they *finally* found a parking spot.

Clearly oblivious to the slight annoyance in her voice, Derek put the car in Park and actually stroked the steering wheel. "But then I wouldn't be able to show this baby off. I just got her on Saturday."

"So you told me already." Twice.

When Derek finished petting his new car, he finally turned it off, got out and came around to Grace's side. At least he opened doors. That was something.

*It's not enough.*

Grace accepted his hand as she got out of the car. But when she tried to pull away, Derek held on tight.

"Come on, honey. You're the other thing I want to show off."

*Gross.* "I'm not an object, Derek."

"What?" He looked down at her. "Oh, right. Of course, not," he said with zero conviction.

They walked to the party and were greeted by their hosts, a lovely couple who had recently built the house. After exchanging pleasantries, Derek made a beeline for the bar, steering Grace in that direction.

It took ten minutes to get a glass of wine in the packed house. Derek ordered a whiskey and practically downed it in one large gulp.

"Might as well get another while we're here," he said and gestured to the bartender. Grace subtly slipped a five-dollar bill into the bartender's tip jar.

They moved away from the bar and made their way into the living room. Derek draped his arm across her shoulders. Grace wiggled, dislodging his arm.

"Hey, did I tell you about my golf game the other day?"

"Yep, you sure did." Another boring story she'd had to endure on the way over. Grace seriously needed to reconsider her rule about giving dates multiple shots. Sometimes you just knew after the first date.

"I was on fire," Derek said, ignoring her reply. Then he went on to recount the "epic round" for a second time. Grace took the time to familiarize herself with her surroundings.

The house was very tastefully decorated in beige tones. The recessed lighting was turned low and jazz music was playing softly in the background. If Grace had to guess, the host had quite the budget at Williams-Sonoma. She'd noticed much of the furniture and decor from the recent catalog.

She craned her neck to get a look at the food table, which was overflowing with different kinds of cheeses and crackers, fruit and crudité plates. She noticed oysters, fresh shrimp and flank steak, and a guest walked by holding a plate with what looked and smelled like lobster mac-and-cheese.

In other words, the party was picture-perfect.

And she was miserable.

When some of Derek's colleagues sidled up to him and

began telling lame, questionable jokes, she excused herself and headed for the food table.

"Hey, aren't you Derek's girlfriend?"

Grace dropped the carrot she was putting on her plate and turned to find a petite woman with long blond hair and a stylish black dress pointing at her.

Grace wouldn't have been surprised if a big, blinking neon sign that said Warning Sign Number One had been hanging over her the woman's head. Before Grace could correct the blonde, she continued.

"I'm Penny. I'm engaged to Brad."

Penny waved a massive diamond ring in her face. While Grace normally took the opportunity to introduce herself and her wedding-planning business to newly engaged people, Penny was rushing forward.

"Derek talks about you nonstop. You should have heard him last Thursday. You know all about Brad's annual cookout."

Grace did not. Then again, she didn't know who Brad was, either.

"Derek is just so excited about your relationship."

"Uh…" Grace found that odd considering this was only their fourth date. The other three had hardly been groundbreaking.

Once again, she felt that neon warning sign blinking away when the chatty woman continued.

"Oh, and have an amazing time in Turks and Caicos! I gave Derek some tips and hot spots. You know that's where Brad proposed."

Nope, she sure didn't. But how could she when she hadn't been aware she was going on vacation with her fake boyfriend.

She decided it was beyond time to offer Derek a piece of her mind. His delusions needed to be set straight. They weren't dating. She wasn't his girlfriend. And there was no

way she would ever consider going on vacation with him—
let alone go out with him again.

Grace could feel herself getting worked up. She should
have never come to this party with Derek tonight.

She heard him laughing loudly and saw a fresh drink in
his hand. *Great. Guess I'll be Ubering back home.*

Although, that was the least of her problems. She could
have been at home, catching up on work or binging that new
romcom series she had in her Netflix queue. Heck, she could
have been watching glue dry and had more fun.

Well, she wasn't helpless. She could walk out of here at
any time.

Mind made up, Grace put her plate on the table, turned…
and ran into a solid wall of muscle.

"Ow," she squeaked.

"Sorry, I didn't see…"

The deep baritone voice caused goose bumps to pop up
all over her arms. Grace inhaled sharply—she knew exactly
whom that delicious voice belonged to. She looked up to find
the one person she actually despised.

"Xander," she groaned.

The surprise quickly faded from his face and his eyebrows drew together. "Grace."

What was with the universe tonight? Was there any other
way this night could suck?

"What are you doing here?" she asked, suspicion in her voice.

She didn't know what it was about Alexander Ryan, but
the man brought out the absolute worst in her.

A frown marred what some people would call an incredibly handsome face. Xander was the best friend of Jack,
Emerson's fiancé. They'd met a few times now and each
time only further solidified the fact that they had nothing
in common.

Actually, there was one thing they shared. An intense dislike for each other.

Too bad. Because if he wasn't so annoying, she might find him attractive. After all, he had classic movie-star looks that certainly turned heads everywhere he went. He was tall and fit, with broad shoulders, hair so thick and dark a woman—well, not her, but some woman!—might love to run her fingers through it and the most mesmerizing blue-green eyes that stood out even more because of the dark lashes that surrounded them.

She had no idea why, but the two of them had been at odds since the moment they'd met. Maybe it was because their professions were polar opposites. Xander was a divorce attorney. She helped couples start their lives together and he helped them end them. Maybe it was the fact that he'd made quick work of dismissing wedding planning the first time they met. Maybe it was his utter self-confidence, which she normally would find appealing in other men, but with Xander it just came off as arrogant.

Or maybe it was that the air became riddled with electricity whenever they were in the same room together. And she didn't have the faintest idea what to do about that.

"Work thing," Xander said, answering her question.

God, he smelled amazing. It was then that Grace realized how close they were standing. And her hand was on his chest. She removed it as if she'd placed it on burning coals, which made Xander grin. A slow and completely knowing grin.

"You look…good," he said slowly. "Really good." His eyes narrowed as he glanced around the room. "Too good for this party."

Was that a compliment or an insult? She never knew with him.

Looked like she'd found one more way to be miserable at this hot mess of a party.

## *Chapter Two*

Xander couldn't wait for this party to be over, and he'd only been here for five minutes. He was an attorney, not a socialite. Yet somehow, attending these events was becoming as common as waltzing into the courtroom.

Not that Xander didn't like a good party. But tonight's soiree was definitely not his idea of a fun time. In fact, he'd been racking his brain and still couldn't remember exactly whose party this was, or what occasion they were celebrating. All he knew was that his boss had "strongly encouraged" him to attend. He'd much rather be at the office finishing up some overdue work and then head to his best friend's bar for a beer and to watch the Nationals game.

Instead, he was at someone's wife's party celebrating… something or other. And he knew exactly how it was going to go. He would make insanely boring small talk with his boss and other coworkers. He would laugh at their spouses' lame jokes. And he would pretend he was having a great time while he perused a buffet of fancy food that would taste exactly like the last buffet at the last party.

He didn't remember any classes in law school that prepared him for this side of law. Schmoozing 101.

The cherry on top of this disappointing cake was running into Grace Harris. Wedding planner, eternal optimist and organizer of unnecessarily extravagant parties to celebrate unions that probably wouldn't last five years.

Grace was best friends and roommates with Emerson

Dewitt, the fiancée of his best friend, Jack Wright. Xander adored Emerson. She was fun and sweet and charming and good-natured. Even though he wasn't a big fan of marriage, if Jack insisted on getting hitched, Emerson was the best woman for it.

But Grace Harris was the complete opposite of the likable Emerson. He didn't know what it was, but Grace had long ago made it known that she wasn't a fan of his.

The feeling was mutual.

It hadn't happened often, but every time they were in the same room together, he could practically feel his blood pressure rising. Something about her brought out the worst in him.

Maybe it was the way she saw everything in life as some kind of movie moment, with a picture-perfect happy ending just around the corner. Plus, there was the fact that she turned up her prim little nose at his chosen profession. Just because she couldn't fathom one of *her* perfect wedding couples splitting up, she was down on the concept of divorce.

Well, she might not like divorce attorneys but that didn't mean people didn't need them.

Still, he couldn't deny that she was beautiful. Truly take-your-breath-away gorgeous. With her long legs and perfect skin and a river of thick dark hair that cascaded down her back, she seemed truly unaware of how exquisite she was. Like tonight. She definitely looked stunning in a cherry-red dress and high heels.

Not that her looks mattered. Her beauty did nothing to offset the fact that they had nothing in common.

Standing in front of him, she forgot about the plate of food in her hand and placed her other hand on her hip. He knew she meant to look annoyed or even nonchalant. Instead, the gesture only further defined her hourglass curves.

"As great as this little chat has been—" Grace gestured

to her plate, which contained one carrot and three pieces of shrimp "—I have people to mingle with."

"Have fun with that. I'm sure you'll find some scintillating conversations at this shindig."

Grace rolled her eyes. "Is there *anything* you enjoy?"

He enjoyed verbally sparring with her because she could always hold her own. Her confidence and refusal to back down was appealing. Plus, her green eyes sparkled with every jab.

Eyes sparkling? What the hell was he thinking? He shook his head and swept his arm for her to walk past him.

"I enjoy a great many things, Grace Harris. Maybe one day you'll find out."

She stepped closer to him. So close that her floral scent teased him. He didn't know if it was her shampoo or perfume or lotion. Not that it mattered one bit. Grace smelled absolutely delectable.

"Oh, I think I know plenty about you now, Xander Ryan."

He didn't back down. He leaned into her. "Astound me."

"You're way too arrogant," she said. "You think wedding planners and weddings are a joke." She took a breath. "If you weren't Jack's best friend and if Emerson wasn't the most important person in my life, I wouldn't even waste my precious time talking to you now."

He pinned her with his best seductive stare and lowered his voice. "But you *are* talking to me now."

She gulped. "Not for long." She broke eye contact and shoved past him.

He couldn't help but laugh. "Oh, Grace," he called.

She stopped and glanced over her shoulder.

"Great running into you."

Again, she rolled her eyes. "Goodbye, Xander."

With that, she continued through the dining room and disappeared around the corner. Xander couldn't help but watch her retreating form, which was just as gorgeous from the back as from the front.

To be honest, he was a little sorry they'd gotten off on the wrong foot. Not that he would admit this to anyone else, but when he'd first seen her, he'd had a visceral reaction like never before, to any woman he'd ever met. It had been as if she'd punched him in the gut. It wasn't just her beauty that had called out to him. It was something else, something indefinable.

Then she'd opened her mouth.

Maybe he shouldn't have made that joke about her planning unions that would inevitably end up in his office. Yeah...that hadn't gone over so well. That was probably when she'd decided that he was an unreasonable, unfeeling person. Well, the thought was mutual. Grace was—

"Xander, welcome."

He turned to see Carl, his colleague at the firm, and had to stifle the urge to yell "aha."

"Hey, Carl. Thanks for the invite."

"No problem. Happy to have you at the housewarming."

*Housewarming—double aha.* It was all coming back now.

"Great place, man," Xander offered.

"Thanks. Make sure you tell Maggie that. She's been stressing about this party for weeks."

"Everything looks amazing."

Carl swirled his drink. "You need help planning a wedding?"

"Huh?" Xander asked, confusion in his voice.

Carl chuckled. "Saw you talking to Grace Harris. Didn't realize you knew her."

"Friend of a friend," he offered. "You know her?"

"A little. I've run into her a couple times. She's here with Derek Whittaker."

*Oh, come on!* Xander couldn't stop his eyebrows from

raising. Derek wasn't one of his favorite people. In fact, he thought the guy was a total jerk. "Seriously? What the hell is she doing here with *him*?"

"Not sure what's going on there to be honest. Derek claims they're dating, but if they are, it's a really new thing."

At that moment, Xander spotted Grace and Derek in the next room. Seemed like Derek only had eyes for Grace. Xander couldn't blame the guy, but still. Yuck. Derek was such an egotistical ass. Someone who took locker-room talk to a whole new level by boasting about his conquests in a little too much detail.

What did Grace see in the guy? Maybe Derek was putting on some kind of facade with her. Maybe he should just go over there and let her know—

"Do you need to get that?" Carl asked.

*Huh? What?* He realized his cell was ringing. "Uh…" Xander stared down at his mother's name. Which was the lesser of two evils? This party or talking to his mother?

Since his night was already a bust, he decided to go for it.

"I do need to take this, sorry," he said to Carl and quickly made his way outside to the long front porch, which was covered with flowerpots.

"Xander, darling, I can't believe I'm actually hearing your voice. I was just telling my stylist the other day that I was sure my handsome yet extremely aloof son was a myth."

He choked back a groan. "It hasn't been that long. I saw you last month." He switched the phone to his other ear and clamped down on the annoyance that had been growing since he'd stepped into this party.

Eloise Ryan elicited a delicate cough, which was her signature way of saying "bull." "That was two months ago and in any case it's quite shameful to not see you more often when you live less than ten miles from us. You should be over here all the time doing your laundry and scavenging for food."

He ran a hand through his hair. "You do realize I'm not a nineteen-year-old college student, right? I'm capable of doing my own laundry, I have a cleaning person and I actually can cook a couple meals."

Ignoring his comment, Eloise continued. "I'd love for you to come to dinner soon. There's someone I'd like you to meet. Someone special. Someone special to me, that is."

If Xander had been a dog, this was when the fur on the back of his neck would stand at full attention. He'd been down this road with his mom before. Come to think of it, he'd been down it with his father, as well.

He took a deep breath and braced himself. "Who is he?"

"His name is Gareth. He's a musician."

Xander paced away from the gray house with tasteful white trim as he spotted some of his coworkers making their way toward it. That was all he needed. People to learn about how dysfunctional his parents were.

"A musician, really?"

"Well," his mom replied in a singsong voice, "he teaches guitar lessons when he's not working."

*At least this one works*, he thought bitterly.

"He's a barista," Eloise said this with the amount of a pride one might reserve for a brain surgeon.

"He works at Starbucks?" Xander said through gritted teeth.

"No, he does not work at Starbucks. He works at a local and very exclusive coffeehouse in North Arlington, smarty-pants. No need to be snobby about it."

Xander ran a hand through his hair again, and then silently cursed himself for messing it up. "How old is Gareth?"

"A robust and mature twenty-four."

Now Xander let out another curse, and this time it was not silent.

"Xander Michael Ryan, watch your language."

"Are you seriously trying to discipline me? You're dating a twenty-four-year-old. Does Dad know?"

"Who knows? He's been spending so much time up in Sag Harbor with his little trollop that I doubt he would care."

And so it went.

Xander's parents had been married for thirty-two years. He'd come along eight months into their marriage. Clearly he'd been the reason they'd gotten hitched. Still, he often wondered if they'd ever loved each other. Had they ever been faithful? As long as he could remember, their relationship had always been contentious. Fighting and cheating and accusations and denials.

He wished he could be truly surprised to hear his mom's latest news but sadly, he was all too used to it. If it wasn't his mom bragging about a new boyfriend, it was his dad gallivanting with someone half his age. Then his mom would retaliate by buying expensive jewelry while his dad would try to one-up her with an exotic trip.

Nothing shocked Xander.

The only question he did have was why had they never divorced. The psychologist he'd been forced to see during adolescence would surely draw a comparison between his confusion over his parents and his chosen profession as a divorce attorney.

"Listen, Mom, I have to run. I'm at a work event."

"You're taking your father's side, aren't you?"

He stifled a groan. "No, I'm not taking anyone's side. But I do have to go."

They said their goodbyes, and Xander actually felt grateful as he ascended the stairs and reentered the party. He was immediately met by Carl's wife, Maggie, who just had to give him a tour of their new house. Along the way he was cornered by his boss and drawn into an insanely dull conversation. Could this night get any worse?

As his boss talked shop with one of his other colleagues, Xander couldn't stop himself from scanning the party, searching for something. Not something. Someone. Someone named Grace. He cursed himself silently. Why was he looking for her? What was this pull between them? It didn't make any sense. She'd made known her feelings for him.

And yet, when he spotted her talking to that jerk Derek, he actually smiled. He could stare at her all day. He was fascinated by the way she carried herself. Her looks made her seem delicate, but she definitely had a pretty strong dose of confidence about her, too.

But as he watched, something caught his eye. Derek was latching on to Grace's arm and pulling her around the wall into a very dark and secluded corner. Xander craned his neck. Even from his vantage point, he could see that Derek's grip was too hard. Grace's smile faltered and her eyes registered anger. Anger and something worse. Fear.

Xander ignored everything around him. Instead, he placed his empty glass on a nearby tray and crossed the room in several fast strides.

It all happened so quickly he didn't have time to register anything. Not the fact that he'd just blown off his boss. Not that he'd been completely rude. Not even that he was interrupting something that was none of his business.

All he knew as he watched Derek's grip tighten around her arm was that Grace might need help.

"Derek, let go," she said.

"You listen to me," Derek said between clenched teeth. His eyes had darkened. Neither of them noticed Xander standing there.

There was still a chance to back out, still a chance to mind his own business. But seeing the expression on Grace's face, he knew he couldn't do that.

In the end, it didn't matter—because Grace brought her knee up to Derek's groin and then quickly and deftly twisted out of his grasp. She twisted his wrist behind his back in some kind of complicated-looking hold.

Before Xander could swoop in and save her, she'd saved herself.

And despite their mutual disdain of each other, he'd never been more attracted to her.

## Chapter Three

*Nothing like breaking out your self-defense skills at a cocktail party*, Grace thought sarcastically.

Thank goodness Emerson had talked her into that self-defense course. And the occasional follow-up class. Grace didn't even want to think how this situation would have ended otherwise. She clamped down on the shiver that threatened to crawl up her spine. While she was holding strong on the outside, on the inside, Derek had really scared her.

She'd informed him that he had no right to call her his girlfriend. That this would be their last date. And that she didn't appreciate his getting sloshed five minutes into a party.

That's when any semblance of charm had vanished from him and been replaced by anger and outrage.

*You have this under control*, she reminded herself. As she tried to catch her breath, she slowly realized that Xander was standing by her side.

"Xander," she growled. "What are you doing?"

He was frowning. "What do you mean what am I doing?" He flicked his eyes down to where she had Derek's wrist in a tight grasp. "What are *you* doing?"

"I'm on a date." *Duh.*

A slow grin spread over his handsome face. "How's it going?"

Her lips twitched. She couldn't help it. "I've been on better."

Derek winced in pain. "Let go of me, you little bitch."

Xander stepped forward and leaned down to get in Derek's face. "Excuse me—what did you call her?"

Without missing a beat, Xander gently took Grace's hand and untangled her fingers from Derek's wrist. At the same time, he used his free arm to bend the creep's arm behind him, far enough to cause just enough pain to get the guy's attention. "She's not your property. And it seems she doesn't want to be, either. So if you ever put your hands on her again, I'm pretty sure she'll do far worse than put you in a basic self-defense hold."

Derck glanced at Grace, who leaned closer and whispered, "I'll use my Taser on you."

The jerk looked like he was about to say something, but she grabbed the purse she'd dropped on the floor and left both men behind. All she wanted to do was get out of there as quickly as possible, go home and get out of this dress. *I mean, I wore Spanx for this?*

But Xander quickly caught up to her right before she could exit the living room.

"You handled that really smoothly," he said, amusement and something else in his voice. Surprise, maybe?

"You think?"

"What I think is that it was impressive. Damn impressive."

Aware that quite a few sets of eyes had turned in her direction and the whispers were beginning, she decided to throw all her attention at Xander. She whirled back to face him. "I've been dating since I was fifteen years old. Do you honestly think this was the first time I've had to deal with some creep? I really didn't need your help, you know." Although, if she were being honest with herself, deep down…she was grateful. Grateful she hadn't had to deal with Derek's brutishness alone.

Even if it had to be Xander, of all people, who'd helped her!

"Well, I... I'm sorry. I just hated to see you being treated that way." His jaw worked, as if he couldn't figure out what to say. "How many creeps?"

She pretended to look at a watch she wasn't wearing. "How much time do you have?"

The party hosts, Carl and Maggie, rushed to her side. "Grace, are you okay? We heard something happened with Derek."

"I'm okay," she said, trying to reassure them.

"You may want to check on Derek, though," Xander added, tucking his tongue into his cheek.

Maggie looked back and forth between the two of them. "Oh, wait, what? What happened?"

Carl was shaking his head. "I knew I shouldn't have invited him. It's just, his boss and our boss," he said gesturing to Xander, "are tight. They all golf together."

"It's okay," Grace said.

Suddenly, all the energy drained from Grace's body. She was exhausted. But she didn't want to be rude, so she said her goodbyes as fast as she could, if a bit robotically.

"I'm so sorry to have caused any kind of scene. I truly am fine, but I'm ready to head home. I've got an early day tomorrow. Congratulations on the new home. It really is beautiful."

Then she made a quick getaway toward the front porch. Once outside, she breathed in the fresh night air deeply, as if she'd been stuck in some kind of hole for the last couple of hours. In a way, she felt as though she had been. But things with Derek were over and she was fine. Just fine.

She sensed Xander before he spoke. His deep voice washed over her like some kind of security blanket. She wanted to feel his arms around her, wanted to hold on tight and forget about this whole horrible evening.

"Grace, are you okay?" he asked. Worry laced that sexy baritone.

She inhaled deeply and then plastered the same smile she used with unruly brides on her face. She turned around to face Xander. "Of course—I'm fine. I just want to get out of here."

Uncertainty filled his eyes. "How are you planning on doing that? How did you get here?"

"Derek drove. But I actually don't live far from here. I'm going to walk."

"Walk? Why don't you take an Uber or Lyft, at least?"

"I think I can make it on my own, Xander," she said with a confidence she knew was false, as she hugged her purse closer to her.

"After what I witnessed tonight, I'm sure you can. But to be honest, I'd feel a lot better if you weren't out on the streets all by yourself." He stared out into the inky black darkness of the night. "If you insist on walking, why don't you at least let me accompany you?"

Was he implying that she was some damsel in distress who needed saving? Sure, she'd been a little nervous there for a second, but she was completely safe now. If she was honest with herself, she longed to find that one perfect person who would always be by her side, to be her knight in shining armor—hell, she'd built a career out of doing that for others. But deep down, well…she knew it wasn't realistic to have a handsome rescuer at your disposal, to swoop in and save you whenever you got into trouble. And she definitely didn't want to cast Xander, of all people, in the role of prince. Besides, she was more than capable of taking care of herself.

She'd certainly done it long enough.

*Then why are you shaking?* a little voice whispered in the back of her mind.

"Look, Xander, I appreciate the offer, but I said I was fine. I think I can manage walking a couple of blocks."

And yet, once again, her mad faded. After all, Xander

was trying to do something nice for her. If it had been any-one else, she would have gladly accepted the offer. So why didn't she want Xander to walk her home?

*Because you don't want to be alone with him.* Really, she was afraid of what she would do *if* she was alone with him.

"Please, go back to the party," she said with little hope he actually would.

Xander turned back toward the house. He gazed at the large picture window of the living room, where people were swirling their martinis and comparing the square footage of their houses. "You want me to go back in *there*?"

"That's what I said."

He gestured between the two of them. "Were we at the same party? And I use the term *party* loosely."

Unable to help it, she smiled.

"Come on." He nodded toward the street. "Let me walk you home. I'll even let you insult me and my job on the way."

"Hmm, tempting." She gave one more glance at the party, where she saw Carl talking to Derek. She shivered.

*You're fine. You handled it.*

Her quick pep talk didn't work. Suddenly, her mind was going through every possible scenario.

"Hey, what's that?" Xander placed a hand lightly on her arm.

She shifted until she was right under the porch light, where she could already see a bruise forming on her arm from that idiot's hand.

"Does it hurt?" he asked.

"It, um, it…"

With that, the last bits of adrenaline left her. Without warning, without a moment to stop herself, she collapsed into Xander's arms.

Xander would have been less shocked if Grace had told everyone at the party that they were best friends.

Truth was, he shouldn't be surprised that Grace was in his arms, holding on tightly. She'd had quite the night. Plus, during their discussion, he'd spotted her shivering.

Still, she'd been so confident, even while handling Derek's attempted abuse. In every interaction he'd ever had with her, Grace had always been completely poised. For once, it was kind of nice to see that armor disappear, though he wished it was for a different reason.

He heard her take a deep shuddering breath and rubbed his hands up and down her back.

"It's okay, Grace. You don't have to worry about him anymore."

After a long moment, she finally straightened. He watched as she pulled herself together, putting on that armor once again. She smoothed a hand over her hair and took a deep breath.

"Thanks, and sorry," she said.

"Sorry? What for?"

A flush crept across her cheeks. "For having to deal with me just now. When I, uh…"

"Had a perfectly natural human moment?" he offered.

As expected, her flush disappeared and she narrowed her eyes. "I just needed a second to gather myself."

"Whatever you say." He grinned, and she made a low sound that actually resembled a growl. "But I'm still walking you home."

It looked like she was going to fight him on it. But then she glanced back at the house and finally nodded in agreement. They descended the stairs of the porch and turned left onto the sidewalk.

"So," she began, "I don't get it. I was at that party on a date. I barely knew those people. But it seems like you do. Is this the type of event you go to often?"

He groaned. "Unfortunately, I do more often than I would like. It's a work thing."

"Your boss requires you to?"

"Let's say he strongly suggests it."

"Ah. One of the perks of working for myself," she said.

They fell into silence for a moment, the only sound the *click-clack* of her heels on the sidewalk.

It was a beautiful night for the first day of October. There was a full moon overhead, lighting the way. The weather was still warm, but a refreshing breeze was blowing through the trees, which were just on the cusp of changing colors.

Xander realized this was the first time he'd ever been completely alone with Grace. Not that they'd spent all that much time together to begin with. But usually Jack and Emerson were around, or they were surrounded by customers at The Wright Drink, Jack's bustling bar in Old Town. "Speaking of being your own boss, how's the wedding business going?"

She sighed.

"What? I'm trying to be nice here."

"You had an attitude when you asked that."

"No, I didn't," he protested.

"There was a tone."

"A tone? Come on."

"I already know how you feel about my profession, Xander. You made it crystal clear the first time we met."

"It goes both ways. You've made it evident that you hate my job."

"You're a divorce attorney. You see the end of marriages every day. What is there to like?"

He shrugged. "There's more to it than that."

"Oh, really? Astound me."

"People come to me when they're ready for a change in

their life. It's not always fighting and yelling. Sometimes a breakup is a healthy thing."

"Oh, please."

"Not everything can be rainbows and lace and tiered cakes," he said.

She threw her arms in the air. "Some of those tiered cakes are really fantastic."

"What's your favorite?" he asked out of the blue. His impromptu question made her halt briefly.

"You'd think it was gross," she answered.

"Try me."

"Carrot cake. I really love it."

*Interesting.* "That's my favorite, too."

"My grandmother used to make it for me all the time. Her recipe is to die for. Speaking of," she said as her phone started playing "When You Wish Upon a Star." "Excuse me." She held her phone to her ear. "Grammy, hi, is everything okay? It's late… What?… Oh, sorry about that. I had to rush from work to this party."

As she spoke to her grandmother, they continued walking. Xander tried to give her some space by taking in their surroundings. The streets had definitely emptied since he'd arrived at the party, but there were still some stragglers out and about. Some were returning from work, others were coming or going to a night out. There was a softball field about a block away and he could hear hooting and hollering right before the crack of a bat and the roar of a crowd.

When he turned back to Grace, she'd ended the call and was putting her phone in her purse. "I'm sorry about that. I talk to my Grammy almost every day and she was worried when she didn't hear from me today."

"That's nice you talk so much to your grandmother. I'm sure your parents appreciate the effort."

She glanced down at the ground, suddenly very interested

in the red brick sidewalk. She had such expressive eyes and right now they were emitting a clear sadness. He wanted to know what had made her feel that way.

Instead, he decided to change the subject. He realized he knew very little about Grace Harris. Other than that she got under his skin like no else ever had.

But suddenly, he really, really wanted to know more.

"What made you go into wedding planning?"

"I've always loved weddings. I even did the Disney internship program back when I was learning the business."

"So you like the planning aspect?"

"I like everything about weddings. My grandmother used to read me all of these wonderful fairy tales. They always ended with a marriage. A perfect happily-ever-after. I guess I just wanted to help others make that happen."

"You seem close with your grandmother."

"She and my grandfather raised me."

He wondered where her parents had been in this scenario.

They continued to walk along the streets of Old Town, which grew brighter and busier as they reached the town center. Xander couldn't help but take it all in. He'd grown up not far from here, in a very large house with acres of lush lawns and gardens. Unfortunately, those lawns and gardens were showpieces and not for playing. That's one of the reasons he'd loved visiting Old Town. The entire area always seemed alive to him. As a kid, he couldn't get enough of the excitement. He could run around the marina and look at the ships docked there. A man would sit on the corner and play his saxophone as people went in and out of the different shops. Street artists would display their work. And at Christmas, there were lights strung across King Street that seemed to go on forever, lighting up the sky.

"I love Old Town at this time of year," Grace said, as if reading his mind.

"I was just thinking the same thing."

She laughed, and he realized he liked the sound of it. It had an almost bell-like quality.

"It feels like there's always something new here," she said.

"Yeah," he agreed. "It definitely keeps you on your toes. But at the same time, I love the old feel of this area."

"Exactly," she exclaimed. "Take this block. Who knows? Maybe George Washington walked down this same street. I know he used to stop here on his way to Mount Vernon."

"It's cool to think about. I love that old-time feel. It's stable."

Stability was not something that Xander had had in his youth. His family was anything but stable. Chaos ran that household more than any one person. Maybe that's why he very rarely made the short trek to the very prestigious mansion where his parents still resided.

"Have you been to that bakery on Princess Street? You know, the one with the amazing biscotti."

"One of my favorite places on earth." His mouth watered just thinking about it.

"The cannoli?" she asked, wiggling her eyebrows and making him smile.

"Ah-mazing."

It had been a couple blocks without any arguments breaking out between the two of them. It was kind of nice, Xander thought. When she wasn't driving him out of his mind, Grace Harris was actually kind of cool to be around.

"Sorry about your date tonight." Xander wasn't sure why he said the words. But he felt like someone should apologize to her. Especially since he knew Derek wouldn't.

She shrugged. "In a way it's my own fault."

"How is it your fault that the jerk grabbed your arm and tried to get rough with you?" His fingers curled into fists as he remembered it.

"No, not that part. Derek is a jerk. But I shouldn't have gone out with him tonight."

"Why did you then?"

"I guess I just wanted to give it one more chance, see if there were any sparks. That's my bad habit. I would have much rather been at home catching up on Netflix."

"I know the feeling. I also like a good night at home. Bum out on the couch. Order some pizza. Or go to a baseball game. What about you?"

"To be honest, I've been working so hard lately I don't even know how to relax anymore."

"What made you start your own business rather than joining an established firm?" He realized he was actually interested.

"I've been working since I was a teenager. For all different kinds of people. The last couple of years, I've been gaining contacts and puffing up my résumé. I decided to make the leap from employee to boss."

"Any regrets?"

"Occasionally." She laughed.

There was that sound again. Something about it had him sucking in a breath.

"My favorite part of being a business owner, though, is that it's all mine." She did a dramatic dancer-turn thing, her hair flying behind her head.

He glanced down at her feet. She was wearing tall strappy high heels. He had no idea how women stood on those in general. But the fact that they were walking over uneven and very old bricks, and she'd just done one hell of a turn, was even more impressive.

"Are your feet okay?"

"Are you kidding? These shoes are fabulous. Any pain associated with them is totally and completely worth it."

As if the universe was ready to disagree with her, she suddenly stumbled as they were turning the corner. She wobbled on her feet for one second, two seconds, and then she was falling. He reached out his arms and grabbed her just before her knees hit the hard sidewalk below.

As soon as his arms went around her, her scent engulfed him. She smelled of orange blossoms. And how in the hell he knew what orange blossoms smelled like was beyond him. Only he knew that it was an amazing scent and he would never eat another orange without thinking about her.

Her arms circled around his neck and he automatically pulled her to him, bringing their bodies even closer together than they'd been earlier.

She had the most intense eyes. They were a beautiful emerald color, and he knew that if he stared long enough he would become completely lost.

"Xander," she uttered, her voice breathy.

"Grace," he replied.

He didn't know what else to say. His eyes flicked down to take in her lips. Her full, very pouty, very enticing lips. Her tongue slipped out at that moment to wet them. He had to clamp down on a shudder. Was it his imagination or had she moved her head closer to his?

The breeze picked up and her hair floated around her head. Somewhere in the distance a dog was barking. And he could hear the usual sounds of nightlife, people talking and laughing as they headed out to a local bar.

Neither of them moved. They stood there on the corner staring into each other's eyes under the full moon.

He realized he wanted to kiss her. He wanted that more than he wanted air to breathe. He began to tilt his head toward her. Her eyelids fluttered, then closed.

All of a sudden, the intrusive sound of a loud horn honking startled both of them. Grace jumped back.

"What the...?"

"Grace," he began, but had no idea how to finish the sentence.

"Were you going to…? I mean were you about to…?"

He ran a hand through his hair. "I—I don't know. I think we were going to…"

She put even more space between them. Somehow, he felt a chill. That didn't make sense. It wasn't even cold out.

"We were going to do nothing," she said adamantly. "*That* can't happen between us."

"Nothing happened, Grace. Don't overreact."

"I'm not overreacting. You almost kissed me."

It was true. He had. "I didn't almost kiss you." He had to save face. "You were right there with me. It was a joint effort."

She held her small purse out in front of her like a shield. Although the only thing the tiny clutch could protect her from was a gnat.

"You know what, Xander? We had a nice walk home. Let's leave it at that. My house is right down the street. I'm fine from here."

He watched her retreating form as she headed down the street. Xander stood there for a long time. Long after Grace ran up the steps to her town house, let herself in and closed the door.

What had just happened between them? He didn't even like Grace Harris. And as far as he knew, she sure as heck didn't like him, either.

Yet something had happened on the streets of Old Town. Just like Grace had pointed out earlier, something was always changing in Old Town.

Too bad change wasn't always a good thing.

## Chapter Four

Change was a good thing. Well, mostly. Usually. In most situations.

Grace scrunched up her nose as she thought about all the things that had been changing in her life lately. Her business was taking off and she was acquiring more clients than ever. That was a good thing. Emerson had met the love of her life and was getting married. A definite plus.

Although…they wouldn't be roommates for much longer. Unless Jack was okay with his wife living with another woman. Not likely.

And maybe their social life had been altered a bit, too. They used to spend their free nights roaming Old Town, popping into fun, eclectic shops, or stopping at one of their favorite bars for a glass of wine.

Now, things were different. She saw less of Emerson, who was splitting her free time between Grace and her fiancé. That's why she knew tonight was important.

They were on their way to Jack's house for dinner. Grace loved Jack. He was funny and smart. Most important, he loved her best friend more than life itself. So Grace couldn't complain about being the third wheel. She was happy to be there for Em.

"It's nice of Jack to spend his night off cooking us dinner."

Emerson made a left turn onto Jack's street. "Don't be too impressed. I'm fairly certain he ordered food in. But I think he's going to try and pass it off as homemade. Or he'll default to the grill."

"I'll take it either way. I'm starved."

It had been another long day. She'd spent hours negotiating a hotel contract with an employee who was not in a giving mood. Grace hoped she never had to coordinate a wedding in that particular location again.

Emerson pulled her car into Jack's driveway. They walked to the front door and Em whipped out her key to let them into the house. Grace smiled as she watched her friend so at ease in her new phase of life.

At least she had a best friend who included her often, even though she had a fiancé. Grace knew plenty of women who turned their backs on their friends when they found "the one." Heaven knew she'd seen her share of Bridezillas who alienated most of their friends before they could pick a color for their wedding party.

"What?" Emerson asked.

Grace gave her a swift hug. "Nothing. Just happy you invited me tonight. I'm glad that the three of us can…" She let her words trail off as something caught her eye on the street. A sleek black Lexus was parked outside Jack's house.

*No. Freaking. Way.*

"Emerson…" Grace had to fight hard not to grind her teeth.

Emerson held her hands up in front of her. "Before you say anything—"

"Like, why is Xander Ryan's car parked here?" She crossed her arms over her chest and began tapping one foot.

"Well, see, the thing is, he's kind of joining us for dinner."

"Kind of? Or is he *definitely* joining us for dinner?" Grace practically growled the words.

"Definitely joining us?" Emerson said hesitantly, her face an example of contriteness if Grace had ever seen one.

"Emm-m-m-m," Grace moaned. A thought occurred and Grace grimaced. "Please tell me that you and Jack are not trying to set us up."

Emerson snorted. "Absolutely not. We've seen the two of you together. Although, physically, I think you'd make a hot couple. But my ears would have to stop ringing from the constant fighting."

"It's not constant…and what do you mean we'd make a hot couple?"

Emerson laughed and shook her head. "Listen, Gracie, you're my best friend. And Xander is Jack's best friend. You guys have to start getting along. You're going to be in each other's lives from now on."

Suddenly, Grace's appetite disappeared. Emerson was right. She was marrying Jack and if Grace wanted to keep having nights like these with her best friend, she was going to have to learn to put up with Xander, too.

She attempted to run a hand through her hair until she remembered she'd thrown it up into a messy bun. And she hadn't touched up her makeup since this morning. Plus, she was wearing loose-fitting boyfriend jeans and an old royal blue top that she'd owned forever and a day. She'd definitely looked better.

*Dammit*. Why in the world was she even caring about her appearance? She glanced back at the Lexus. She didn't want to answer that.

"Come on, Gracie. Do it for me. Ple-e-e-ease."

"Fine, I'll have dinner with the evil one." She quickly ran her index fingers under her eyes, hopefully ridding herself of any errant eyeliner and mascara. She wished she had her makeup bag.

Emerson chuckled. "He's not evil, Gracie. Just give him a chance. He's a really nice guy. Trust me."

She did trust Emerson. But as far as Xander was concerned, she'd have to get some examples of him being a good guy first. Walking her home one time hardly constituted Man of the Year. Especially when he'd tried to kiss her.

It was days later and she still wasn't sure what irked her more—the fact that Jack had tried to kiss her, or her disappointment that he hadn't.

They pushed open the door, crossed the threshold, and were immediately engulfed in a flurry of fluffy exuberance. Jack's dog, Cosmo, was so excited to see them that he couldn't seem to wag his tail fast enough. His entire little twenty-five-pound body was shaking back and forth. How could anyone stay in a bad mood when they were greeted with this?

"Hello, handsome boy," Emerson said in a high-pitched voice which seemed to set Cosmo over the moon. She scratched and rubbed him as he attempted to lick her anywhere he could reach.

Then it was Grace's turn to shower Cosmo with affection. "What a good boy. Who's a fluffy puppy," Grace said in her own version of a doggy-voice.

Cosmo sat and held his paw up.

"Oh my goodness, you can shake. What a good dog. What a smart doggy."

Emerson snorted. "Oh yeah, he's smart all right. He knows he gets a treat if he does that."

Emerson dropped her purse onto the console table by the door and grabbed a treat out of a jar next to it. Then she led Grace through the house, as Cosmo happily marched alongside them. Grace had been to Jack's a handful of times. It used to belong to his father, before he passed away, and it was definitely a bachelor pad done up in dark colors. Although, now that she glanced around, she could see Emerson's hand. Colorful throw blankets and pillows were in the family room and she noticed some of Em's favorite artwork hanging on the walls. There was a lamp in the corner that used to sit next to the chaise in Emerson's office. And in the living room, she spotted a pair of Em's flip-flops peeking out from under the couch and her sweater tossed over a chair.

She could hear the men's voices coming from the kitchen. Sighing internally, she vowed to give Xander a fair shot and actively work to change her impression of him.

"I couldn't be happier to see a marriage end. Their breakup was a long time coming," Xander said as he leaned back against the counter, a beer bottle dangling from his fingers.

Grace gritted her teeth. Then again, maybe first impressions were right for a reason.

They entered the kitchen and Jack's face lit up as he took in his fiancée. Cosmo danced around, clearly thrilled that something new was happening. Then he made a beeline for his water dish.

"There's my bride-to-be," Jack said, oblivious to Grace's boiling temper. He scooped up Emerson into his arms.

"I like the sound of that," Emerson said and kissed him.

"Where's my kiss?" Xander asked.

Jack's arms tightened around Emerson. "Get your own."

Emerson laughed and squirmed out of Jack's arms to hug Xander. Then she gave Grace a pointed look that clearly suggested she should play nice.

Did she not just hear Xander dissing marriage?

She smiled. "Hi, Jack." She sighed. "Xander."

"Grace, great to see you again. And so soon." He was all confidence and ease. He must have come straight from the office because he was still wearing a suit. Although, he'd removed his jacket and she noticed a baby blue tie hanging over one of the chairs in the kitchen. The sleeves of his dress shirt were rolled up, revealing strong, muscular arms. Arms that looked like they could wrap around her tightly and securely, protecting her from the evils of the world.

*Stop it!* She needed a drink. "Twice in one week. Am I lucky or what?"

"Yeah, or what," Xander replied, sarcasm dripping from his voice.

"Drink?" Jack asked, quickly holding up a bottle of wine.

"Yes," Grace and Xander said at the same time.

Jack laughed and uncorked the wine, then poured a glass before handing it to Grace, who took a long swallow to steel her nerves. Xander, too, seemed to accept another beer from his friend rather eagerly.

"What's on the menu, babe?" Emerson asked.

"I thought I would grill."

Grace exchanged a glance with Emerson and they both started giggling.

"I think we missed something," Xander said.

"Better to simply nod and smile," Jack said in a stage whisper.

While Emerson and Jack talked about the food situation, Grace couldn't keep her eyes off Xander. And wasn't that just annoying? Why did the man have to be so attractive? Couldn't he have scales or rampant acne or something? No, he just had to possess one of the most handsome faces she'd ever seen. He could pass for a movie star. Instead, he was an arrogant jerk.

"I'm going to fire up the grill," Jack announced. "Em, I know you were out there last weekend. Did you move the grill tools?"

"Yep, I was rearranging."

"Uh-oh, there she goes, Jack. Your independence is dwindling away." Xander poked Emerson in the side and she poked him right back.

"Shut up. I had to rearrange some stuff so we have room for the lounge chairs."

Jack turned from the refrigerator, burger patties in hand. "See…wait, what? I don't have lounge chairs."

"You will on Thursday." Emerson gave him another kiss. "That patio space is awesome, but you weren't utilizing it."

Jack laughed as he and Emerson headed out the sliding glass door to the patio in question, Cosmo happily following in their wake.

Xander called after them, "It all starts with some lounge chairs."

And then they were alone in the kitchen. Grace decided to look at everything but Xander. She took in the counters that Jack had recently replaced with a light gray granite. She noticed the cabinets that Emerson wanted to paint white. She even looked down at the worn-in pair of Sperrys she was wearing on her feet.

"So," Xander said.

"So," she countered with an eyebrow quirk for good measure.

Then, silence. They both stared at each other, then she rolled her eyes. Finally, he cleared his throat as if to speak. She could tell he was choosing his words carefully. "I happen to really like Emerson."

She crossed her hands over her chest.

"Seriously," he said. "She's awesome. And I was only teasing them."

"Hmm." Grace supposed she could take his word for it.

Xander leaned back against the counter and took a long swig of his beer. Grace's gaze was drawn to his lips. Those smooth lips that had almost been on hers the other night…

"Moving on," he finally said, cutting off *that* train of thought. "How was your day, dear? How's the wedding biz?"

Grace mirrored his stance by leaning up against the opposite counter. "Quite busy, actually."

She talked about a recent bridesmaid brunch she'd put together on the fly, as well as an upcoming bridal shower and two different bachelorette parties. Then she regaled him with the hotel contract woes she'd experienced today, and threw in a couple of nightmare stories of her dealings with florists for good measure.

Finally, Grace finished her wedding overload. She had to bite her lip from laughing at Xander's blank expression.

"Well," he said. "That's a lot for one day in a couple's life. I mean, I've been to plenty of weddings, but I never really thought about what went on behind the scenes. You really take on a lot of responsibility."

"Some couples want to make sure everything is perfect," she said with a shrug.

He nodded his head. "I guess. But it still seems like a waste of money."

She growled under her breath. "It's a special day. Think about your own wedding."

He let out a mirthless laugh. "Never going to happen."

"What do you mean? You're never getting married?"

"Nope. I don't believe in marriage. At all."

The look on Grace's face was priceless.

He would have laughed. But Xander had a feeling if he did, Grace wouldn't take too kindly to it. Telling this particular wedding planner that he didn't believe in marriage was probably akin to telling a cartographer that he didn't think the earth was round.

Yes, he wanted to get under her skin, but he happened to be telling the truth. After his experience with his parents, not to mention what he saw every single day at work, there was no way he could be all rah-rah about the idea of weddings and commitment. Because he didn't believe in them at all.

Frankly, he never should've started this conversation. Jack hadn't mentioned Grace would be coming to dinner until he'd already arrived and popped open a beer. Smart man. Once they were comfortably catching up on the latest Nationals win in the kitchen, there was no way he could make an excuse to get out of the evening. And it definitely hadn't taken long for the usual disagreements between him and Grace to surface. Xander considered himself a fairly patient man, yet when this raven-haired beauty came around, any semblance of patience flew out the window.

Even with the shocked expression on her face, she was beautiful, especially with her thick, dark hair piled on top of her head. He'd love to get his hands in it and mess it up even more. Watch it fall around her heart-shaped face before he kissed her...

Her mouth opened and then closed as she seemed to struggle for words. "You really don't believe in marriage?"

Jack walked into the kitchen, heard Grace's question, looked between the two of them, grabbed another beer and quickly backed out.

Xander shook his head. "No."

"No marriages?"

"Nope."

"I'm not just asking about you personally. I get that marriage is a personal choice. By all means, feel free to not want to get married."

"Thanks," he said dryly.

"But you don't believe in marriage at all? Like, between any two people?"

"That's what I said."

"But...*why*?"

Xander had the impression that he could have said he

threw kittens over cliffs and she would have reacted less harshly. If she only knew what he'd grown up with. What he continued to see transpire between his parents—two people whose marriage was the foundation for some of the worst fights on the planet.

"It's hardly a shocking thing, Grace. A lot of people don't believe in marriage."

"Oh, yes, I see that every day in my line of work. That's why I have a waiting list to plan those big, fancy parties that you think cost too much money."

"They do cost way too much. Come on, it's one single day."

She shook her head and ignored his comment. "What about children?"

He shrugged. "I don't know if kids are for me. But I don't have anything against children. Besides, you don't need a piece of paper to have children."

"What about commitment?" she persisted. "Showing the person you love that they can trust you?"

"Again, you don't need that little piece of paper to show you're committed. If you even choose to be 'committed.'" He used air quotes when he said the word *committed*.

Her eyes narrowed and she pointed a finger at him. "What does that mean?"

"You can say some words in front of your friends in a church or a hotel ballroom or under a chuppah or wherever. Doesn't mean squat. That's what *I see* every day in *my* job."

"Not everyone gets divorced."

"Half of married couples split up."

"Half of married couples stay together," she countered, stepping close to him. They were nose-to-nose. "Do you have any idea how much love I see on a daily basis?"

He had to stifle a groan. She was beyond delusional.

"Love? You see wedding dresses and china patterns and dollar signs."

Her mouth dropped open and an indignant huff escaped. "You know nothing about my job. I happen to see couples who want to celebrate their love with the people in their lives." She returned to the other side of the kitchen, picked up her wineglass and took a long drink.

"Oh, please," he snorted. "Just this morning, I met with a couple who had one of the biggest, grandest, most extravagant weddings of all time. You know when they got married? Three years ago."

Grace narrowed her eyes. "Is that the marriage I overheard you talking about? The one you were so thrilled had ended?"

Xander felt his face fall. He would have cast his gaze to the floor, only there was no way he was letting Grace win this round. She was glaring darts at him, but she had no idea what she was talking about. There was a very important reason why he was happy to assist with this particular divorce.

"No," he said slowly. "What I saw today was the end of one of the worst unions I've ever witnessed."

He'd known Jess since college. She'd dated his roommate. She had always been a fun, outgoing and kind person. The relationship with his roommate hadn't worked out, but Jess had stayed in touch, even after she got married to someone else. She'd always been a bright light in his world.

Unfortunately, Xander had no idea that while she was smiling on the outside, her world had been falling apart.

Xander ran a hand through his hair. "Today, I finalized a divorce for an old friend. Her scumbag of a husband had been abusing her, both physically and verbally."

Grace gasped.

"She'd felt trapped, alone," Xander said.

"That's awful." She bit her lip. "I'm sorry. I guess… I can see why you were so happy it ended."

*Progress*, he thought. "I'm not a monster, Grace. I don't believe in marriage, but that doesn't mean I get some kind of perverse joy out of seeing people's happiness crushed when a union ends."

She put her wineglass on the counter. He thought she was going to walk to him, but in the end, she stayed where she was. She did meet his eyes though.

"I'm glad to hear that. I guess it's the optimistic part of me that wishes everyone could be happy all the time."

Xander actually loved that aspect of her. Sometimes, he wished he could be more positive in life. Only, he'd seen too much, witnessed too many unhappy endings.

"Unfortunately, life isn't a fairy tale, Grace. The world has evolved."

"You might not believe it, but I do understand that." She offered a small, sheepish smile. "I guess I just hate the idea that someone might never plan to find your soul mate and fall in love. That you'll never know what it feels like."

She raised her arm in emphasis, and Xander's eyes were drawn there. He searched, but didn't see any of the bruise from the other night.

"Now that we've talked about my unwillingness to settle down, I wanted to find out how you're feeling after the other night."

Confusion crossed her face. "The other night? You mean, when we ran into each other?"

"Yeah."

"When you almost kissed—"

"When Derek was a total jerk to you." Xander pointed his beer bottle at her arm. "I see the bruise has faded."

"Ah." Her cheeks reddened. "*That* part of the other night."

"Well, yeah. I don't know him well, but what I have heard of Derek hasn't been all that complimentary."

What he didn't tell her was that their almost kiss had shaken him up more than he wanted to admit. Even now, he had to actively work to keep the desire to press his lips to hers from surfacing again.

"Has he contacted you since the party?" Xander asked, pushing the unbidden need to the back of his mind.

She shook her head. "Nah. I don't expect him to."

"Let me know if you do hear from him."

Her eyes widened. "Why?"

"Because I don't want him bothering you."

"Are you trying to protect me, Xander Ryan?"

Was he? Xander wasn't sure. All he knew was that seeing Derek grab Grace had set something off inside him.

"I think you proved the other night that you are perfectly capable of protecting yourself."

She grinned. "Thank you for saying that."

"You're welcome."

Silence engulfed the kitchen for a few moments. Something had just shifted between them. Xander could feel it as clearly as he felt the cold bottle of beer in his hand.

"Are we getting along right now?" Grace asked.

"We might be."

"Shocking," she said, her eyes sparkling.

"It is shocking," he agreed. "Who would have thought that we could stand in Jack's kitchen together and have a civil conversation."

Grace raised her glass. "How about a toast to getting along for five whole minutes."

"I'll drink to that."

He closed the gap between them, his gaze shooting down to Grace's enticing lips. He could see her chest rising and falling as he tapped his beer bottle to her wineglass.

Xander wasn't sure how they came to this point. Maybe—just maybe—they'd learned something about each other tonight. All he did know—and he knew for damn sure—was that just like the night he'd walked her home, he wanted to kiss her more than he wanted air to breathe.

The door opened and the aroma of charred beef and cheddar cheese wafted over to them. Cosmo let out a little *yip* right before Emerson poked her head in. They sprang apart, guiltily. "Hm, I don't see any blood or guts," she said. "Is it possible you two are getting along?"

"We even toasted each other," Grace said.

"The temperature did drop pretty drastically outside," Emerson said.

"Really?" Grace asked.

Emerson rolled her eyes. "Oh yeah, when hell froze over."

"Clever," Xander said.

"Thank you. In any case, the food is ready. Want to come out here and eat? Cosmo is dying for one of us to drop something."

"I got your back, Cosmo," Xander said.

Slowly, Xander made his way onto the patio. Grace was facing the other way and Emerson was whispering something to her.

"Are we one big, happy family yet?" Jack asked wryly. He swiveled and cocked his head at his fiancée and Grace. Then raised an eyebrow in question at Xander.

Xander shrugged. He may not have the answers to life's biggest questions, but there was one thing he knew for sure. Things had just gotten interesting between him and Grace.

## Chapter Five

Grace hated fidgeting when she was with a client. And today's client was no ordinary bride. It was Emerson.

She wanted everything to be perfect for her best friend. Even if she had to work twenty-four hours a day from now until the wedding, she would make sure that every table looked perfect, each flower petal was pristine and all *i*'s were dotted on the invitations even if she had to write them out in her own hand.

If only she could concentrate.

She'd been having issues all week. Unfortunately, she knew the cause. *Xander Ryan.* She blew out a long, frustrated whoosh of air.

"You okay over there?"

She offered Emerson a smile. "Sorry. Yes, I'm fine. Where were we?"

"We were right in the middle of squashing my most recent wedding-induced panic attack."

"Right." Notebook poised on her lap, Grace nodded at her best friend. "Okay, let's review the choices that you've made already. I'm telling you, you're ahead of the game."

"Venue, check." A big smile blossomed on Emerson's face. "I still can't believe we got that space. It's my dream wedding site."

"A spring wedding in a vineyard," Grace said dreamily. "It's going to be amazing."

Emerson scrunched up her nose. "You don't think the

timing is weird? I know most people do the whole autumn-in-a-vineyard thing."

Grace squeezed her hand. "The timing didn't work out unless you wanted to wait another couple of months."

"No way," Emerson said. "I'm way too excited to become Mrs. Wright."

Both women laughed, as they did every time Emerson's new surname came up. After all, who couldn't help grinning at the thought of marrying the real Mr. Wright? "That's what I thought. Spring wedding it is. The cherry blossoms and dogwoods will be in bloom. It's going to look beautiful."

Grace continued down her checklist. "You've picked your dress. Which the groom has already seen," she added as she narrowed her eyes at Emerson.

"I'm sure he doesn't remember that. And, anyway, it's not like he's seen me all done up and ready to walk down the aisle."

"Fine, fine. I'll let it go for now. But you have to promise not to break any other cardinal prewedding rules."

"Hate to break it to you, Gracie, but Jack and I have already done it."

Grace stuck out her tongue. "How about you commit to not spending the night before the wedding together?"

"I'll consider it."

"Let's see. The save-the-date cards are ready to be mailed." Grace scrolled down the page in her notebook. "You've already picked out the invitations. We've narrowed it down to two caterers. Jack is taking care of the honeymoon."

"We have to pick out your maid-of-honor dress," Emerson said excitedly. "My mom got in this really cute line of bridesmaids' dresses last week at her shop. We should get over there and take a look."

As Emerson began leafing through a bridal magazine and dog-earing pages with different dresses she liked, Grace's mind began to wander again. To her dismay, it found its way right back to Xander.

She was still processing the two times she'd seen him recently. How she'd been so upset at *not* being kissed by him after that awful party!

Then there was the other night at Jack's house. They'd started off at odds, but in the end, something changed.

Hearing about his client had affected her. Not to mention his concern over her after the party. Not even the hosts had called or emailed to make sure she was okay.

Xander was right. He wasn't a monster. Far from it. He was actually turning out to be…kind of a nice guy.

She felt so confused. Did she like Xander or not? Did she want to kiss him or not?

"I almost kissed Xander," Grace blurted out.

Emerson stared at her for a long moment before blinking once, twice. Then she coughed delicately and closed the bridal magazine. "I was going to bring up the idea of tea-length bridesmaid dresses but let's talk about your news instead."

Grace dropped her head into her hands and groaned.

"I assume we're talking about the one and only Xander Ryan, your nemesis here?"

Grace acknowledged this with a long groan. Was he still her nemesis? "I don't even want to talk about it."

"Uh-uh, you have to spill now. You can't drop a bombshell on me like that and just clam up. Let's start with where this almost kiss happened. Was it the other night at Jack's?"

Grace sat up straight. "Actually, I saw him at that horrible party I went to with Derek earlier this week."

Emerson held up a hand. "Excuse me, that was several days ago. Why didn't you tell me this earlier?"

"I was in shock, I think. I don't know what happened."

"Take a deep breath. Then start with how you got to the

point where you almost kissed him and end with why you didn't."

So Grace did. She spilled every detail she could remember. When she finished, Emerson just sat there.

"Em, say something."

Emerson ran a hand through her curly hair. "It's a lot to take in. I'm processing." She sighed. "I really wish I could have seen you take that creep down."

"It was pretty amazing. But, back to the issue at hand. What about Xander?" Grace asked impatiently, fidgeting in her chair.

"What about him?"

Was Emerson serious right now?

"He walked you home, which I give him high points for. You guys finally started getting along and then you tripped, he caught you and there was an epic romance moment."

"An almost moment because nothing actually happened."

Emerson studied her for a long time. Grace actually began squirming in her chair.

"You sound disappointed that nothing happened."

Grace's mouth dropped open and Emerson laughed. "Stop laughing at me. You're my best friend and you're supposed to be supportive."

"I am. I just don't get what the problem is. Xander is a great guy. I know a ton of women who would kill to go out with him. He's stable. He has a great job."

Grace grumbled at that.

"He's successful. He's really funny when you get to know him. He has great taste in best friends." Emerson got the gooey face she usually did when talking about her fiancé. "And, he's hot."

"He really is," she said without thinking.

Emerson's eyebrows went up.

"Well, I'm not blind," Grace said defensively. "He's incredibly attractive."

"I'm glad to hear that." Emerson avoided eye contact. "Because Jack is going to ask him to be his best man."

Grace shrugged. "I figured as much."

"So you're okay walking down the aisle with him?"

"What am I? Five? Of course I'm okay."

Emerson took a big breath. "Then you also won't mind planning a couples' shower with him?" She popped up out of her chair. "Want some coffee?"

Grace's head started spinning. "Wait, what did you say?"

Emerson paused and slowly turned back around. "Jack and I decided that instead of having a separate bridal shower and bachelor party that we'd like to have a couples' shower with all of our friends and family in one place."

"O-ka-a-a-y," Grace said slowly. "That's a good idea. Very modern. I like it."

"And…we'd kind of like for the two of you to plan it together." Emerson bit her lip and scrunched her nose.

The gesture would have been endearing if Grace hadn't gotten the sudden urge to throw up. "Both professional-wedding-planner Grace and best-friend Grace are offended."

"Gracie, don't be like that."

"Come on, Em. I can handle planning a shower all on my own, thank you very much. I don't need Xander in the mix, getting in my way and messing up my flow."

"Listen, this was Jack's idea. He's not having a bachelor party and he thought it would be nice for Xander to have something to do besides just standing next to him on the big day. Plus, Xander knows all of Jack's friends."

Grace narrowed her eyes and crossed her arms over her chest. "I'm going to ask you this question for a second time. Are you and Jack trying to play matchmaker? Be honest, Emerson Rose."

"No, we are not. Trust me," she said with emphatic eyes. "Although, you did almost kiss the other night."

Grace stuck her nose in the air. "I regret telling you that now."

"No, you don't." Emerson crossed back to her, grabbed her hand and pulled her to her feet. "I know this isn't ideal for you, but please try. For me? I promise he'll be at his best." She put on her most winning smile.

Grace blew out a puff of air. "Fine. I'll plan a shower with Xander."

Emerson was right—this was not going to be her favorite part of planning the wedding. In fact, spending more time with Xander was sure to have her reconsidering her entire profession.

"You want me to do *what*?"

Jack had to be kidding him. What did he know about throwing a wedding shower?

Xander stared at his best friend and attempted to display his most pained face. Jack appeared unmoved.

"Seriously, Jack."

Jack was working behind the bar at The Wright Drink, the bar he'd inherited from his father. Even though the bar was located in the heart of Old Town, the place had fallen on hard times during Jack's father's illness and become a less-than-desirable hangout spot. But once Emerson came along, she'd helped Jack turn the business around. Now, it was bustling every night of the week. Jack hosted trivia nights, ladies' nights out, sporting events and even a board-game challenge. Plus, Emerson booked plenty of special events, like parties and receptions.

Xander enjoyed coming here. There was a large square-shaped bar in the middle of the room, plenty of high and low tables, a stage and dance floor for karaoke and great framed photos of Alexandria along the walls.

"I am being serious," Jack said. He poured a beer from the tap and slid it over to Xander's waiting hand.

"Why can't you just have a bachelor party like every other man on the planet?"

Jack flipped a rag over his shoulder. "Because I don't want a bachelor party. Besides, once Em explained what a joint shower could be like, I thought it sounded fun. Plus, her mom was pushing for an engagement party and Emerson didn't want one. Too fussy for her, and frankly, for me, too. So this was a decent compromise."

Xander took a good, long swallow of his favorite beer. Too bad it did nothing to calm his nerves. "I don't even know where to start in planning something like this. Do I have to find a venue?"

Jack shook his head. "We want to have it here."

"Okay, but what about everything else? Do I have to do invitations or is this an e-vite situation? And who do I invite? How do I know what kind of decorations to use? Do you need decorations for this thing?"

Jack held his hands out in front of him. "Whoa, slow down."

"Order up."

Jack turned to grab the plate of chicken fingers and sweet-potato fries the waiter had placed on the bar. "Your food's ready." He snatched a rolled napkin with silverware and made his way out from behind the bar. "Oscar, you got this?" His bartender nodded.

Jack gestured for Xander to follow him to one of the tables. Xander took his beer and sat across from his friend. He dove into the chicken fingers.

As he ate, he began to reiterate why he was not going to be a good party planner. "I'm happy to be your best man but hanging up streamers and blowing up balloons isn't my thing."

Jack snorted. "Streamers? Balloons? This isn't a party for a bunch of five-year-olds. Anyway, I thought you might have this type of reaction," Jack said, snagging a fry. "That's why Emerson and I are bringing in some help for you."

Okay, this was something he could get behind. Help. Someone who planned parties. Someone who especially knew how to plan wedding-type parties. He froze, his hand pausing in midair with a sweet-potato fry in his fingers.

*Oh, crap.*

"Wait a minute…" he began.

"You just said you didn't know what you were doing."

"Don't tell me," Xander said, a pleading note entering his voice.

"She's the maid of honor."

"Stop." Xander threw down his fry. "Not her."

"Grace is a professional wedding planner."

She was also the star of his recent dreams. Ever since he'd walked her home after the party, he hadn't been able to get her out of his mind.

She'd looked amazing in that killer red dress with the sexy-as-hell heels. Her long hair was begging for him to run his fingers through. And those legs… All he could imagine was them wrapped around him.

Then there was the fact that she'd been able to hold her own with Derek. Grace Harris was anything but vulnerable. And damn if that didn't turn him on. Which was exactly why he shouldn't plan this party with her.

Xander noticed the door open and Emerson waltz in, with Cosmo at her side. She beamed at Jack and then leaned down and undid Cosmo's leash. The perpetually happy dog bounced right over to them while Emerson stopped to say hi to some people at a table near the entrance. Cosmo stood on his hind legs, leaning on Xander's thigh. His little brown nose was twitching as he took in the scent of food.

"You're lucky you're so cute." He broke off a small piece of his fry and gave it to the dog. Cosmo devoured the fry in one gulp and then again turned expectant eyes on Xander.

"Dude, I just gave you something. Jack, you need to teach this mutt to—"

He broke off when he noticed his friend wasn't paying the slightest bit of attention to him or his dog. Instead, he was staring at Emerson. Xander wouldn't have been surprised if hearts had poured out of his eyes.

Jack had found a life partner. Someone who would stay by his side forever. Xander couldn't help but think about his parents, married for over thirty years and no sign of true emotional connection between them. No evidence—other than him, anyway—that they'd ever really cared about each other. Togetherness wasn't always a good thing.

There was always the option of divorce. He wasn't sure why his parents had never pursued it, but if something went off the rails between Jack and Em, there was an escape clause. What would the happily-ever-after-believing Grace say if she knew he was considering her best friend and divorce at the same time.

"I can't work with her," he said abruptly to Jack, who snapped to attention after making moony eyes at Emerson.

"Why not?"

"Because—because…" he stammered like a petulant child. Jack raised an eyebrow. "Because I don't like her."

"Name one thing you don't like about her." There was a challenging gleam in Jack's eye.

"Just one?"

"Come on."

"Get out," Xander said and took a big bite of his chicken finger to buy himself time.

"I'm serious. Name one thing about Grace that rubs you the wrong way."

The room suddenly felt hot. Xander refrained from loosening his tie.

Jack pointed at him. "You can't do it."

"Give me a minute."

"I'll give you twenty. But I don't think that will help."

Realizing Jack wasn't going to let this go, Xander struggled to come up with a reason why Grace drove him nuts. Besides the fact that she just did.

"She's so…"

"Yes?"

"She's too perfect. What's with the optimism? How can someone be that happy all the time? It's not natural."

"Too perfect? Are you kidding me? You're really stretching now."

Cosmo batted his paw against Xander's leg. "Don't you feed this dog?"

Jack beamed. "He enjoys chicken tenders."

"And fries, and all other food in the world apparently." He slipped another piece of fry to Cosmo who gobbled it right up.

"Back to Grace."

Xander shook his head.

Jack offered a smirk. "You force my hand."

Xander narrowed his eyes. "Meaning?"

"Time to call in the big guns." Jack turned toward the bar, where Emerson was now getting a drink from Oscar. "Hey, babe, can you come over here for a sec?"

Xander leveled a hard stare at his friend. "That's low, man. You know I can't resist her."

He thought about spending hours with Grace planning this party. In any other situation, he would go for it. If he was attracted to a woman, he'd simply ask her out. With Grace, it was different. Xander knew what he wanted out of life. Or, more accurately, what he didn't want. His life path would never mesh with Grace.

Emerson made her way to their table. She set down her glass of Scotch and kissed Jack. Then she took a seat between the two of them. "What's going on?"

"Xander doesn't want to plan our couples' shower."

Emerson made her pretty eyes go wide and batted her lashes. "You don't want to help us out? You, the best man. In our special time?"

"No, see, that's not what this is about. Stop looking at me like that," he said to her. "Seriously, you're killing me."

Jack laughed. "Seems like Xander here is afraid to work with Grace."

Emerson nodded knowingly. "She is pretty scary."

"I don't know what's more frightening, all that pink she wears or those tiny purses she carries around. I wouldn't want to plan a party with her, either."

Xander stifled a laugh. "Stop making fun of me. I'm serious. I can't do it with her."

Jack and Emerson paused, mischief dancing in both their eyes.

"They have pills for that," Jack said.

Xander threw a fry at him. "Shut up."

"How about you do it for me?" Emerson said, suddenly turning serious. "Listen, I'm worried about Grace. I've thrown this wedding at her last-minute and given her practically zero time to plan it. If I was anyone else, she would have turned me down. She has so many other brides to handle. And my sister, well, she can't help out at the moment."

He groaned. "Come on, Emerson…" But he realized she meant it—for once, it did sound as though Grace was overwhelmed. Especially after she explained how much goes into one wedding the other night. Not only does she put together all the details for a wedding, but she also does showers and bachelorette parties and brunches and more. And really, how hard could it be to plan a couples' shower? "Fine, fine. You win. I'll help plan the party."

"Only if you want to," Emerson said, making Jack chuckle.

"You play dirty," Xander said to his friends, then downed the rest of his drink. He was going to need the fortification if he was about to work side by side with Grace.

Then again, he thought…what could happen?

## Chapter Six

"Is this a good time?"

A few days later, Grace paused outside Jack's bar with her hand poised on the door handle. Sophie Miller, one of her younger brides, had just called out of the blue. Never a good sign. Neither was the anxiety Grace detected in Sophie's voice.

"It's always a good time to talk to you," Grace said, trying to add as much enthusiasm as she could to her voice.

"I'm so sorry to call without warning or anything."

Grace wasn't sorry. In fact, she was downright giddy about it. She wasn't a procrastinator by nature, but she definitely appreciated the delay today.

She stepped to the side of the door to allow two women to enter the bar. Glancing in the window, she couldn't miss Xander sitting at the corner of the bar.

It had been more than a week since she'd seen him. Although, she'd been thinking about him plenty. Not long after she learned of Emerson and Jack's desire for a couples' shower, Xander had texted her. He'd asked her to meet him at the bar to start talking about the shower. She'd suggested meeting at her office—her turf—but Xander insisted they'd be more comfortable at Jack's bar. To Grace's mind, it was completely unprofessional. Still, she made exceptions for her clients all the time.

But Xander wasn't a client.

He was a man that she was growing more and more attracted to.

Well, he could wait a little longer. She had a bride to talk to.

"You never have to apologize, Sophie. That's what I'm here for. Now, what's going on?"

"I think I'm making a mistake." This statement was followed by the distinct sound of sobs.

Grace took a deep breath. She'd dealt with plenty of cold feet. There was usually something bigger going on. Even though Sophie was only twenty-four, she'd been nothing but cool and collected in their dealings so far.

"Oh, Sophie, what would make you say something like that? You and Adam are perfect for each other. I knew it from the first time I saw you together."

Grace meant every word. She'd worked with plenty of brides and she'd never seen a groom look at his fiancée the way Adam did. A wave of jealousy washed over her. She could only wish and hope that someday she would find a man who would gaze at her in the same way. Like she was the only woman on the planet.

Grace pivoted toward the window. Xander was watching her from the bar, wearing an expression that she couldn't decipher. But his gaze was intense, and if she wasn't mistaken, she saw a tic in his jaw. She didn't want to acknowledge the way her pulse had picked up. Instead, she gestured to her cell phone and held up a finger so he would know she needed a minute. Then she promptly turned her back and returned to her conversation with Sophie.

Ten minutes later, she had a happy bride again. As she suspected, Sophie wasn't nervous about marrying Adam. Rather, she was anxious about moving to New York City right after the wedding and starting a brand-new life in a new city without any friends or contacts. Grace threw out a couple ideas to help her with the adjustment and by the end of the conversation, Sophie was laughing again and talking excitedly about her upcoming wedding-dress shopping.

Grace made her way toward the bar and joined Xander, making sure to leave a seat between them. She made a big show of pulling out of her large tote the various catalogs, magazines and other material she thought would be helpful in planning a shower.

"Thanks for finally joining me," Xander said in lieu of a hello.

"Sorry for keeping you waiting, but I got a business call on my way into the bar."

Xander's eyebrows went up. "Did I just get an apology?"

Grace offered him her most winning smile. "Even princesses make mistakes."

Jack sidled up to them then. "Hey, Grace, how are you?"

"Great," she said. "Look at this place. You're pretty packed for a random Wednesday."

Jack grinned. "I'd love to take credit, but it was all Emerson. Just wait until Saturday, when we have our Oktoberfest extravaganza. Are you going to stop by?"

"Of course. I wouldn't miss it."

"Great. What can I get you to drink?"

"A glass of that house red I like, please."

Jack reached for a wineglass. He jutted his chin in Xander's direction. "Need a refill?"

"Nah, I'm good. I just want to get to planning this super-fun party."

Grace didn't get it. The last time they'd been together they'd gotten along. Maybe not at first, but eventually. She didn't really want to plan the shower with him, but she was hopeful they would at least get along. Instead, she heard the sarcasm in his voice. Heck, the people playing darts in the corner could probably hear it. Grace decided to take advantage.

"If you'd rather not plan the shower, I'm perfectly willing to do it all by myself." She crossed her fingers under the bar, hoping he'd take the bait.

Xander eyed her suspiciously, but after a blatant don't-even-think-about-it look from Jack, he backed down.

"After all, this is my job. And I'm getting paid to do this," she added.

A wrinkle formed on Xander's forehead. "Hey, that's right. I'm not getting paid."

Jack poured Grace's wine and then punched Xander in the arm. "Have you ever paid for a drink here? Not to mention all the food I give you."

Xander raised his glass in toast to his friend. "Touché."

"That's what I thought. I'll just leave you to it, then."

Jack moved down the bar, taking orders and starting tabs. Grace took a fortifying sip of wine and then faced Xander.

"So," Xander said. "Where do we start?"

She flipped open her notebook. "I've already talked to Emerson. She gave me a bunch of dates that will work."

She showed Xander the list and the two of them consulted with their own planners and schedules. Ten minutes later they had a date. Progress.

"We know they want to have the party here," she said. Grace had been in this bar plenty of times, but she still took a moment to look around the space and visualize possible ideas.

"Awesome," Xander said. "So we can use the food they already serve here. Chicken fingers, burgers, poppers..." Xander trailed off as she sighed loudly. "What's wrong with french fries and wings?"

"Nothing, when you're watching the game," she said.

"I don't get it," he said, frowning. "They want to have the

party here in this bar. Doesn't that lead you to believe they want the food, too?"

"This location means something to the two of them," Grace said, with little patience. "They met right out back."

Judging by his confused expression, Xander wasn't following. She'd need to break it down. "This is more than a wedding shower. It's an engagement party and shower and celebration of Em and Jack's upcoming nuptials all rolled into one. We have to keep that in mind. We also need to remember that her parents will be attending, as well as many elderly guests. That means we need to create a party that is fit for someone in their twenties, as well as an octogenarian."

He nodded slowly. "So no burgers?"

She laughed lightly. "We also have to keep the couple in mind."

"Jack and Emerson like burgers."

She waved her pen at him. "Exactly. That's why we have to compromise."

He straightened in the high-back bar chair. "Pigs in a blanket. You can't go wrong with pigs in a blanket."

She stared at him for a long moment.

"Let me guess. Pigs in a blanket aren't fancy enough for you."

Grace rolled her eyes. "Actually, I've had pigs in a blanket at many events. However, Emerson hates hot dogs."

"Ah." Xander actually looked sheepish. "Sorry. I thought you were going to have something disparaging to say about pigs in a blanket."

She sighed. Loudly. "You're not getting it. This isn't about me."

Xander gave her a look that screamed he wasn't buying it.

Was he really under the impression that she planned weddings for herself? That every event reflected her wants and needs? She rolled her shoulders in annoyance.

"Seriously, Xander, do you honestly think I would let my personal opinions and preferences interfere with planning an event for someone else? That would be incredibly selfish."

Jack paused in front of them. "How's it going?"

"Great," Xander said.

It was clear he meant it. Xander thought this conversation was going well. He didn't get that he'd actually just offended her.

"I wouldn't go with 'great,'" she said.

Confusion flashed in his eyes. "Why not?"

"Um, pigs in a blanket?" She didn't notice any recognition in Xander's eyes. "Insulting me?"

"When did I insult you?"

She let out a sound that could only be called a *guffaw*. "Um, just now."

Jack grinned. "Well, sounds like everything is moving along." Then he hightailed it to a group of new customers in need of drinks.

"How did I insult you?" Xander repeated.

She shook her head, hoping the motion would ease the headache that was starting. It didn't.

"Forget it."

Xander shifted in his chair to face her. When he did, his leg brushed hers. Grace immediately felt a rush of electricity.

"No way," he said. "If I hurt your feelings, I want to know why, and how. Because that wasn't my intent."

Grace sat back and sipped her wine. Maybe she was just being too sensitive.

On the surface, she knew she put her all into each and every wedding she planned. No matter what, she would go the extra mile for her brides.

But, there was always something in the back of her mind. A seedling of doubt that she wasn't, well, good enough.

When she looked over and saw the concern on Xander's face, she felt a little embarrassed.

"You know what?" she said. "I've had quite the day. I think I just overreacted to something you said. We have a lot to cover tonight. Let's get back to it."

He didn't say anything for a few moments. Finally, he said, "If you're sure."

"Of course. Now, as I was saying, this party is about Jack and Emerson, who both happen to favor comfort foods. That's why I was thinking we could have a mashed-potato bar."

"What's that?" She saw the flash of interest in his eyes.

"A bar with mashed potatoes and all the fixings. Bacon bits, sour cream, chives, cheese. You know, the stuff you put on top of mashed potatoes. Maybe we could even do something fancy, like truffle oil. For protein, I was thinking sliders."

"I thought you nixed the burgers."

"I nixed the idea of bar burgers. Sliders are fancier. They're also easier to eat in a cocktail-party setting. We could do beef and chicken. Oh, maybe a prime rib option."

"What about vegetarians? I know Jack's cousin is one, and a friend of ours from high school is vegan. We should offer cauliflower steaks, or something like that."

She was impressed he thought of that. "Good idea."

He seemed pleased with the praise. "Thank you."

She continued. "And for entertainment—"

Xander snapped his fingers in front of her face. Grace sat up straight.

"A hypnotist. Wouldn't that be awesome?" He beamed.

"Why would we have a hypnotist at a wedding shower?"

"Why not?" he asked, seemingly truly perplexed.

"Because it's weird."

"Would you rather have a stripper?"

Grace clamped down on the urge to roll her eyes. "I'm sure Emerson's mom would really love watching a stripper." She finished the last gulp of wine.

Xander started laughing.

"What's so funny?"

"I was just thinking about Emerson's parents watching a stripper. You gotta admit that would be worth the entrance price."

"Are you going to take any of this seriously?"

"I am taking it seriously. The problem is that you're no fun. Just because you've planned dozens of these—"

"Exactly." She pointed at him. "This is my job. You might want to follow my lead."

"And you might want to stop being so bossy. Just because you're a phenomenal wedding planner doesn't mean you can do and say whatever you want." He cocked his head at her, almost in challenge.

Grace had a retort all ready to go. Instead of spitting it at him, she froze.

Xander said she was phenomenal at her job?

"I thought you didn't really get what I do. How do you know if I'm good at it or not?"

He shrugged. "I'm learning more each time I'm with you. From everything I've gathered so far, you really know your stuff."

Her heart melted a bit. His compliment meant the world to her. In fact, being praised for her work actually made her happier than being told she was beautiful or hot.

For years, men always seemed to focus on her appearance. But knowing that Xander wouldn't say something if he didn't mean it, well, that went a long way.

She tried to say something, but her mouth was suddenly dry. Xander, on the other hand, didn't seem to have the same problem.

"Our friends wanted us to work together, so you might as well get used to me. And it wouldn't kill you to use one or two of my ideas. Like the hypnotist. Maybe you could just trust me on that? I promise I wouldn't suggest something that would ruin my best friend's shower, Grace. In spite of what you might think of me, I do give a damn about Jack's happiness."

"You think I'm good at my job?" She knew she sounded dumbfounded, as if no one had ever complimented her before.

"Uh, yeah. You're great. You're also funny when you're not yelling at me. And you're beautiful, too."

Just like that, her excitement came to an abrupt end. *Beautiful*. Yuck.

He paused, his eyes defiant. "Yes, beautiful. For the record, I think that's what you are. Take a moment to digest that."

When he was around Grace, he completely lost…well, everything. His rationality, his good sense and apparently his inhibitions.

Despite the empty chair between them, they were both leaning forward, almost nose-to-nose. The night had been a ping-pong game of emotions. They argued, they agreed. It was getting to be exhausting.

He knew he probably shouldn't have called her beautiful. But, come on. Her smile, her hair, that heart-shaped face and lush body. Who in the hell wouldn't call her beautiful? He bet everyone did.

Yet, something had changed. She'd seemed so excited when he told her she was a phenomenal wedding planner. Then he'd called her beautiful and her face fell. He saw what he thought was hurt flash. Some emotion he couldn't quite identify had filled her eyes, making them seem even more mysterious. Her face was awash with vulnerability. Xander didn't get it, though.

He was in trouble. Yep, he was smitten with Grace. And Xander didn't use the word *smitten*. He needed to win back the upper hand.

"Don't go thinking anything because I said you're beautiful, by the way." He knew he should stop, but found that he just couldn't. "I've dated a lot of beautiful women, you know. Not that we're dating," he added hastily.

He wanted to punch himself. But any pain only lasted for a moment. Then that fighting sparkle returned to her eyes and Grace looked angry. "There's a lot more to a woman than the way she looks. Playboys like you usually don't get that."

*Playboy?* He didn't think so. "I am not a playboy. I know there's more to a person than their appearance. I happen to treat the women I date like gold."

She snorted. "I'm sure you do. Right before you dump them after the fifth date." She sat back and tapped a manicured finger against her lips. "Or do you even give them the courtesy of a breakup? I bet you just ghost them."

That was simply insulting. "Listen, I have never—"

"Xander, Grace," Jack said suddenly and firmly.

They both turned and shouted at him. "What?"

Jack did not seem pleased. "Guys, as much as I've enjoyed this little preschool pissing match, do you think you can tone it down? You're starting to drive away paying customers."

Xander nodded toward Grace. "If someone would stop making assumptions—"

Grace slapped her hand on the bar. "If someone would stop making juvenile comments—"

"Enough," Jack interrupted. He pointed toward the back of the bar.

"What?" Xander asked. "Are you sending us to time-out in the corner?"

Jack rubbed a hand over his face. "No, I'm sending you to my office. At least we won't be able to hear you arguing from back there. Now go."

Grace opened and closed her mouth, clearly shocked that she was being punished. She was probably that little girl who never once got reprimanded in school. If Xander wasn't so annoyed, he'd have laughed.

She grabbed her ridiculously large tote, plus all of the wedding-related books and magazines she'd brought and the two of them headed toward the door in the back corner with the antique sign that read Office.

Jack's office wasn't very large. There was enough room for a wooden desk and chair, a filing cabinet, a coat stand and one other black metal chair that looked incredibly uncomfortable. The windowless room had a musty smell that reminded him of a cross between a library book and a sewer.

"I can't believe he sent us back here." Xander threw his arm out to indicate the room.

Grace dumped her purse and supplies on Jack's desk. "If you would have just come to my office like I suggested, we wouldn't have to be in this stuffy room."

"Are you telling me that you would rather sit at the desk in your office than come to this fun bar and have a drink and some mozzarella sticks?"

She made a big show of searching the tiny space. "I'm sorry. I'm not seeing any drinks back here, let alone any appetizers."

He clapped his hands together slowly. "Aren't you hilarious?"

"I don't know why you're so annoyed with *me*. This is all your fault."

He stepped toward her. "How is this my fault? We were both fighting out there. I should add that I'm not even really sure what we were fighting about."

She closed the distance between them and crossed her arms over her chest. "You started it. You were purposely goading me."

"No, I wasn't. You've made up your mind where I'm concerned and you're not interested in anything I have to say."

She gasped and he could tell his words struck a nerve with her. "Would you stop fighting with me? Please, Xander? I don't want to argue with you, really."

"You want to stop fighting?" he asked as he jutted his chin in the air in challenge.

"Yes."

"Fine. You got it."

He grabbed her upper arms, pulled her to him and crushed his mouth down to hers. She gasped and pulled back. There was a moment—a long, heated moment—where they simply stared at each other. And then she threw herself back at him and their lips sealed together again.

God, she felt good. She melted into his arms and he was only too happy to gather her even closer to him.

Her lips were soft and he could taste the red wine she'd had earlier. He moved his hands to frame her face so he could deepen the kiss. She sighed deeply and he took advantage of the gesture to slip his tongue into her mouth.

Finally, after all that fighting, the two of them were in sync. In fact, they couldn't get enough of each other.

He hadn't made out like this since he was a teenager. Their mouths were greedy and their hands moved everywhere. He wanted to feel as much of her as he could. He ripped his lips from hers so he could go on a tour of her jaw, her chin and down the column of her neck. She moaned as he nipped her earlobe and then fisted her hands in his shirt to bring him even closer.

He returned to her mouth and once again they kissed each

other as if they were the last two people on a planet that was about to explode.

This wasn't supposed to happen between the two of them. Yet, being like this with Grace felt more right than anything had in a long, long time.

Xander had no idea how long the kiss lasted. Nor did he have any inkling as to why they both seemed to end the kiss at the same time. They stared at each other, twin expressions of shock and awe. Her arms were wound around his neck and his were holding her tight. They were both breathing heavily.

He struggled for something to say. But before he could get the words together, Grace jumped back as if she'd been burned. Unfortunately, her bracelet caught in his shirt and as she went backward, so did he. They crashed into Jack's coatrack, causing it to fall to the floor as they lurched into the wall.

Grace cursed, a surprise coming from her. Xander stifled a laugh. He pushed off the wall, bringing her with him. Then she worked on getting her bracelet untangled from his shirt. Finally, they were able to separate.

She touched a hand to her lips and he attempted to straighten out his now-wrinkled shirt.

"You kissed me," she said. Her eyes held an accusatory gleam that he didn't care for.

"You kissed me, too," he countered.

"No, I didn't…" Her chest fell as if all the air had been let out of her body. "Okay, yes, I did. I really did."

She put a hand to her forehead in a very damsel-in-distress type of way. Xander wondered if she was going to pass out, which would be a first for him. Although, something very masculine inside him reveled at the idea of his kiss giving her that reaction.

"Are you okay?" he asked.

She dropped her hand. "Of course I'm okay." Her jaw

worked as she clearly tried to make sense of something he couldn't quite understand himself. "I have to go," she said abruptly.

"What?" He blew out a whoosh of air. "I hardly think you need to leave just because we—"

"Don't say anything." She began searching the space, turning in circles.

"What?" he repeated. "Grace, there's no need to be embarrassed."

She whipped back to him. "I'm not embarrassed. One little kiss is barely enough to make me feel uncomfortable." She grabbed all of her belongings.

"Then why is your face red?"

"Because...it's hot back here. That's why. And, anyway, your face is flushed, too. Maybe you're the one who's embarrassed."

He jammed his hands in his pockets. "I wouldn't say that's how I'm feeling at the moment." What he was experiencing was an extreme case of lust. He wanted a woman who until very recently he'd despised—and he could have sworn she felt the same way.

Or maybe he'd wanted her all along.

Everything was all mixed up. He was beginning to see how hard she worked at her career. He'd watched her defend herself. He knew how loyal she was to her friends. Basically, his initial impression of her being some kind of princess with unrealistic views of the world had completely changed.

Xander took a moment to remember the first time they'd met. It had been in this very bar near the front door. He'd almost run into her and he'd been speechless. He'd met plenty of stunning women in his life, but there was something about Grace that jumped out at him.

Naturally, they'd started fighting before they'd even been

properly introduced. And they hadn't stopped until they'd made out a couple minutes ago.

"I have to get out of here. I have work to do." She was scrambling now with her belongings.

"Grace, wait. You don't have to leave."

She paused at the door, yanking on the doorknob. He crossed to her and lifted the fallen coatrack, which was blocking the door.

"We haven't finished our planning," he said in a desperate attempt to keep her there. And why did he even want her to stay?

"I think we need a break. We did a lot tonight." Her gaze flicked down to his lips and she let out a shaky breath. "I'll email you more details."

When she made a move to open the door, he stopped her with a hand to the door. He kept his arm anchored there and leaned down to whisper in her ear. "I don't think a break is what the two of us need."

After a moment of silence, she turned to meet his eyes. "That's what I'm afraid of."

With that, he removed his arm and she shot out the door. Xander watched her flee the bar, making eye contact with Jack, who threw him a questioning look. Xander shook his head.

He meant what he'd said to Grace tonight. They didn't need a break, but damn if he didn't want to admit what they did need.

She said she was afraid. He knew the feeling.

After having a taste of Grace Harris, he knew he needed more. And that scared him more than anything.

## Chapter Seven

Grace was furious. She stomped up the steps that led to the front door of her town house. Heat permeated every inch of her body and she knew her temper was barely contained.

She jabbed her key in the lock and let herself in. Then, as if suddenly deflated, she sunk back against the door.

She placed a finger to lips that were still tingling. Closing her eyes, she replayed the kiss. The amazing, wonderful, mind-blowing kiss.

"No," she said adamantly. "No, no, no."

Even if Xander Ryan had the best damn lips on the East Coast, there was absolutely no reason for him to kiss her like that.

Or had she kissed him? She guessed they'd kind of kissed each other.

More like they'd sort of dove for each other.

She groaned and banged her head against the door. Now everything seemed so blurred. First they'd been planning, then they'd been fighting, next they'd been banished and finally their lips had locked together like there was no tomorrow.

She shook her head. It didn't matter who started it. What mattered was that it had happened. She detested Xander. He was pessimistic and snarky and—and...totally different than what she'd originally thought.

After all, he'd paid attention to her while they talked about the shower. He offered good suggestions. Maybe not the hypnotist, but the vegetarian options for sure.

And he'd complimented her. On her job.

Of course, then he'd thrown in that comment about her looks. They always did.

"Ugh."

The two of them were complete opposites and they had no business making out. She would just have to make sure that it didn't happen again. Ever. In fact, she would take over Emerson and Jack's shower completely. Surely if Emerson knew how worked up she was, she'd understand. Totally. She was her best friend.

Determined, Grace entered the town house and began stomping up the stairs to their living area. Except for the shower and the wedding, she would never have to be in close proximity to Xander Ryan again.

"I can't step foot in the same room with that man ever again. He's horrible…"

Her words trailed off as she turned the corner into the living room. Emerson was sitting on the floor, tears streaking down her face. She held her cell phone in one hand and a tissue in the other.

Any and all thoughts of Xander, kissing or anything else, simply slipped out of her mind at the sight of her friend in distress. "Oh, my god, Em. What is it? What's happened?"

Emerson waved her phone in an erratic manner. "Winery. We lost it. They had a flood and they'll be closed for events for over a year." She hiccuped as another tear fell.

Grace dumped her purse and tote on the nearest chair and slid down to the floor to join her friend.

"One more time," she said encouragingly.

"The flood and the rain and now I can't get married."

She ran a hand down Emerson's hair, trying to soothe her. "Everything's going to be fine, Em."

With that, another round of tears began and Grace jumped up to grab a box of tissues from the bathroom.

She rejoined Emerson on the floor, pushing the tissues at her. Then Emerson handed her phone over and Grace saw that Emerson had been reading the *Washington Post*. She scanned the article but wasn't getting why it had made Emerson so upset. It was about a vineyard that had flooded due to the recent heavy rains they'd had.

The DC area was notorious for getting the tail ends of Atlantic hurricanes, which meant buckets of rain. Because of that, the vineyard where Emerson was set to hold her wedding had flooded. The article described massive damage that would take months, if not years, to fix.

Emerson sniffled. "I randomly saw the article so I called Michael at the vineyard. He confirmed it. The place is in ruins. The main structure will need to be rebuilt."

Emerson buried her face in a tissue.

"They're estimating a year to fix everything enough to meet health codes and inspection. That means they're pushing all events back. The earliest we could get in would be almost two years from now." She slapped a hand on the floor. "Two years! Gracie, I don't want to wait two years to marry Jack. I'd marry him tomorrow if we could."

"I know, I know. I understand." A bevy of ideas began taking shape in her mind. She reached for the notepad and pen they always kept on the end table close by and began scribbling.

"Here's a list of the other venues you liked."

Eyes still watering, Emerson perused the list. She pointed at one of the names. "They're booked solid for the next year."

Grace tapped her pen against another name on the list. "And this one won't work, either. Remember, the setup didn't mesh with what you wanted."

More tears leaked out of Emerson's eyes. Grace hated seeing anyone in pain, but especially her best friend. Emerson had always been more like a sister, and after everything she'd been through, she deserved the best wedding imaginable.

"Don't cry, Em. We're going to fix this. I promise. Just give me some time."

"What are you going to do?"

"Call in the troops. We need backup."

An hour later, Jack, Emerson's sister, Amelia, their parents and even Xander all sat in their living room as Grace explained the situation. Emerson was still weepy and Jack kept his arm firmly around her shoulders.

"Is there any recourse we could take?" Mr. Dewitt asked.

Grace shook her head. "Not really. Not against Mother Nature. Besides, the vineyard is trying to make it right with all of their clients." Grace had spent twenty minutes on the phone with them to make sure she completely understood the situation.

"Then our options are to either wait two years to get married," Jack said as Emerson let out a gasp, "or to find a new venue."

Grace pointed at him. "Right. I say we go with option two."

"There's always the bar," Jack said, more to Emerson than the rest of the group. "I know it's not the most romantic place in the world but I'm sure we could make it work. And we met right behind it."

Emerson kissed him lightly. "I love you," she whispered. "I guess the bar could work, but I'm not sure our whole invite list will fit." She sighed. "It's—it's just not what I had I mind."

"The wedding was going to be beautiful," Mrs. Dewitt said from across the room with a sigh.

"And it still will be beautiful and wonderful and magical,"

Grace said. She didn't like the use of the past tense or the way everyone's faces had fallen. "We only need to find a place."

"But, Gracie, we both know how vineyards fill up months in advance."

True, but she wasn't ready to throw in the towel.

"You really want to get married in a vineyard?" Xander asked.

He'd been silent since he'd arrived with Jack. Grace had done everything in her power to ignore him. Because each time she so much as glanced in his direction, she remembered the feel of his lips on hers and her heartbeat sped up.

Emerson nodded and Xander rose from his spot on the couch. "I know a guy. Give me a minute." He walked out of the room and headed toward the kitchen, his cell held firmly in his hand.

Jack let out a small laugh. "He always knows a guy."

Someone brought up the idea of a boat and they discussed a couple of the hotels in Old Town. Grace was watching Emerson's face and she could tell that each suggestion was met with less enthusiasm than the one before. All Grace could do was stay positive and keep everyone's spirits up while she tried to figure out what to do.

"We're all set. I have a solution," Xander said with a grin as he walked back into the room. Every head turned in his direction.

"You've saved our wedding?" Emerson asked with doubt in her voice.

"You bet. Isn't that the best man's job?"

*Not really*, Grace thought. Although, now that she was thinking about it, she was impressed that he'd come over. He didn't need to be here. In fact, with his distaste for weddings, it was shocking he was trying to help at all.

"Has anyone ever heard of a vineyard out in Virginia wine country called Hart of the Hills? It's out past Front Royal."

Grace exchanged a look with Emerson. Of course, they'd heard of Hart of the Hills. It was one of the best vineyards in Virginia. The grounds were stunning with amazing views. They offered tastings, but never events.

Xander continued. "I happen to know Max Hart."

"How do you know the owner?" Jack asked.

"I handled his divorce two years ago."

Grace rolled her eyes and Xander took notice.

"I will have you know that Max is much happier now. He reconnected with his high-school sweetheart. They're living together and running the vineyard."

"How does this pertain to our wedding?" Jack asked.

"Max agreed to host your wedding at the vineyard."

Silence fell upon the room for a long moment. It was broken by Emerson's high-pitched squeal of joy.

Everyone began talking at once. Finally, Grace jumped up and shouted above the crowd.

"What are you talking about, Xander? Hart of the Hills never does events. I check in with them every couple of months."

"And they're not going to do any events in the future. Max is making a special allowance for you."

"Why would he do that?" Emerson asked.

"Because I explained your situation to him. I told you, he's a friend of mine."

Emerson ran to Xander and launched herself in his arms. "Oh, my god, thank you, thank you, thank you, I love you, I love you, I love you." She plastered a loud, smacking kiss on his cheek.

Jack laughed before grabbing her hand and tugging her back to him. "Hey, hey, I get the kisses." He grinned at Xander. "But for making her happy, I might have to get up and make out with you."

"Then I shudder to think what you'll do when I tell you

this next part. Max isn't asking for any money for using the space. He would just like you to give a donation to his favorite charity."

Grace's mouth had fallen open. She couldn't believe what she was hearing. An absolutely perfect wedding venue for free. Not to mention, her best friend's tears had dried up and she was smiling again. Xander had saved the day.

Jack wasn't the only one who wanted to kiss him. Grace gulped. But the kind of kissing she wanted to do definitely required an empty room.

Xander pushed a hand through his hair, his smile fading a bit. "There is one hiccup."

"Uh-oh," Amelia said, sitting forward.

"It's not too bad, I promise," Xander said. "Max and his girlfriend, Betsy, are taking the trip of a lifetime. They're going around the world. So they won't be around for your wedding date. But they did have an alternate date."

"Great, we'll make it work," Emerson said.

"I like the positive attitude, Em," Xander said. "They offered up the place for this weekend."

Grace blinked. Emerson's mouth fell open again. Mrs. Dewitt put a hand to her mouth.

Grace broke the pregnant silence of the room. "You did tell them this weekend was a little too soon, right?"

Xander leveled a look at her that read as a big, fat *duh*. "What do you take me for? Of course, this weekend is too soon."

A collective sigh of relief filled the room.

Xander's chest puffed up. He looked prouder than a four-year-old who'd colored inside the lines. "That's why I told them three weeks would be fine."

"Three—three? Three weeks to what?" Emerson asked.

"Three weeks to the wedding."

Jack sat forward. "As in, we'll get married three weeks from this weekend?"

Xander grinned. "You. Are. Welcome."

*Oh. My. God.*

Emerson put her head between her legs. "I'm gonna throw up."

Xander's face fell. "What's wrong? I thought you would be happy."

Jack was rubbing Em's back. "Dude, I don't know much about weddings and even I know you can't plan one in three weeks. That's a really tight time frame."

Xander looked hurt. Hurt and confused. Grace would have hugged him if her heart wasn't beating a million miles a minute at the prospect of planning a wedding in three weeks.

"But...you've got the whole team together, don't you? Grace is a wedding planner and Emerson's an event planner and Mrs. Dewitt owns a bridal boutique."

Emerson smiled weakly at Xander. "I love that you're trying to help us, but three weeks really isn't enough time."

Just as Xander began to nod his acceptance of the statement, Grace stepped forward. Her mind was moving at lightning speed. She tried to sort through a list of items to do, like flowers, centerpieces, getting a caterer, the wedding cake... A plethora of possibilities began to come together in her mind.

"Actually, it might be," she said.

Everyone turned in her direction.

"Might be what?" Xander asked.

Emerson once again lost the color in her cheeks. "No way, Gracie. Three weeks."

"Three weeks and a handful of days. I think we can do it," Grace said confidently.

Mrs. Dewitt stepped forward. "I agree with Grace. We

have to work together. There's going to be a lot of late nights and a lot of favors called in."

"Mama, you can't be serious."

"See, Em? Even your mom agrees."

Amelia stepped forward. "What about you, Grace? Don't you have a ton of weddings right now?"

Fall had become a prime time for weddings in recent years. The truth was she did have two weddings between now and what could be Jack and Emerson's wedding date. Mrs. Dewitt mentioned late nights and Grace definitely saw herself pulling some serious all-nighters.

She glanced at Emerson, who was watching her with a mix of expectancy and hope. She'd do anything for her best friend.

"I have a couple of weddings, but most of the legwork is done." She bit her lip, took a deep breath and addressed the room. "We can do this. Like Mrs. D said, we just need to work together."

Xander met her gaze and held it. He smiled and nodded his head. He seemed impressed with her, and that had a feeling of pride taking over.

Mrs. Dewitt joined her and squeezed her hand. "I agree with Grace. I will handle all of the wardrobe—Emerson's gown, the bridesmaids' dresses and the tuxes."

Grace nodded and turned to Amelia. "Amelia, what's your schedule like at the moment?"

Amelia seemed surprised that Grace was asking. "Um, it's fine. Light, normal."

Amelia worked in Mrs. Dewitt's bridal shop.

"Great, I can use your help on about a million different things."

Emerson stood up. "We really need to drive out to Hart of the Hills and tour the space first."

"You're right." Grace would need to get Max's contact

information from Xander. Then she would give him a call first thing tomorrow morning.

"No worries," Xander said. "I told Max we would come out on Friday at eleven."

"We?" Grace asked.

Xander faced her and lifted an eyebrow in challenge. "Yes, we."

Grace put her hands on her hips. "Why would *we* need to go out to the vineyard?"

"Because *we* are the one with the personal contact. It's appropriate for me to go."

Amelia tried to interject but Grace and Xander were on a roll.

"Yes, but *you* are not planning the wedding. That's *my* job. I've been on plenty of site visits and I think I'm perfectly capable of orchestrating this meeting."

He stepped toward her. Against her will, her eyes flicked down to take in his lips. Lips that only a couple of hours ago had been plastered on hers. She thought she heard his intake of breath. Was he thinking about their kiss, too? Was it having the same effect on him as it was on her? Or was she simply another set of lips for him to kiss and walk away from?

"Would you stop being so stubborn, Grace?"

"Only if you stop being so pushy."

Jack shimmied his body in between the two of them. What had happened to all the space between them? she wondered.

Standing between them to keep them apart, Jack whistled. "Time-out, you two. We really need to stay focused here."

Grace flushed. Jack was right. They were awfully short on time, and she really would have to be on her game to pull off the best wedding ever for her best friend.

Maybe she was being a bit ridiculous. After all, Xander had gone to the trouble of getting the most incredible venue—and the most unattainable one!—booked. If he insisted on coming for a tour, then so be it. She would be way too busy concentrating on all of the other details to notice him, anyway.

Grace swallowed her pride. "Are you sure you can take the time away from your job?" she asked Xander.

"I'll make it work."

She nodded. "Jack, Em, does Friday work for you guys?"

"Absolutely," Emerson said, tucking her hand into her fiancé's.

Grace nodded again. "Then it looks like we'll be going together."

Everyone began talking excitedly. Mrs. Dewitt and Amelia were eagerly discussing the bridesmaid dresses they had in the store's inventory. Emerson hugged her dad. Jack offered to go to the kitchen and grab drinks for everyone to toast the saving of the wedding.

Grace hung back in a corner of the living room, her mind spinning with lists and agendas. The next three weeks were going to be brutal. No way around that. But at least her best friend was happy and that made Grace ecstatic.

Plus, throwing a wedding together in three weeks' time would really prove that she was an above-average wedding planner. She desperately wanted to excel.

"You sure you can handle this?" Xander asked quietly.

Her first inclination was to snap at him. But Grace reined in her temper. Adding to her stress was the thought that Xander was going to be an apparent constant presence in her life. Especially after that kiss.

"I'll be fine."

"I want us to be fine, too," he said earnestly.

She searched his face for signs of sarcasm but found nothing but a stoic man waiting for her answer. "Of course," she said quietly.

"Truce?" he asked, sticking his hand out.

She eyed his hand for a moment as if it would jump up and bite her. Finally, she acquiesced and slipped her hand into his. Something electric traveled up her arm and over her body.

She swallowed deeply. "Truce."

Somehow, she suspected this truce wouldn't last long. Or maybe she was afraid of what would happen if it did.

## Chapter Eight

Grace arrived at Hart of the Hills fifteen minutes early. She'd sampled their wine before, but never been to the actual location where it was made. Even from her seat in the car, she could tell that it was an absolutely stunning venue. The rolling hills of the Shenandoah Valley served as the backdrop, while rows of grapevines surrounded the main building. At the end of the large parking area was a flower-lined path that wove its way up to a two-story wooden house with a wraparound porch that overlooked the vineyards. It had large windows and a welcoming blue door.

"Gorgeous," she said into the quiet of her car. Emerson and Jack were going to love this place.

While she waited for the bride and groom, she took a few moments to go through emails and voice mails in her car. When she was done with that, she tucked her iPad and phone into her tote bag and double-checked her makeup and hair in the rearview mirror.

She'd decided on her favorite pair of wide-legged black trousers and a fitted pink blouse that had an attached belt that closed into a large bow at her side. She'd kept her makeup light, just a light rose-gold shadow and her favorite blush-colored gloss on her lips—perfect for meeting the winery owners. Part of her hair was braided across the crown of her head, disappearing into the waterfall of the rest of her long tresses.

Perhaps she'd put a little more time and thought into today's ensemble. She only wanted to look good since they were on a site visit. It had nothing to do with the fact that Xander would be there. Nothing at all.

A few minutes later, Jack's truck pulled into the spot next to her car, and she waved through the window at Em and Jack. They all got out and greeted each other.

"Oh, my god," Emerson said excitedly. "Look at this place."

"It's amazing, right?" Grace said.

"I guess I'm going to have to continue giving Xander freebies at the bar," Jack said with a laugh. "He's really saving us here."

Speaking of, where was the savior? She checked the time on her phone. They still had a few minutes. Emerson was practically dancing around the parking lot. Grace laughed and pulled her by the hand.

"Come on. Xander can meet us inside. Let's go check this place out."

The three of them walked along the path. Emerson stopped to admire the different colored mums that lined the walkway. They climbed the two stairs to the large porch and pushed their way into the building. A jingle sounded as they crossed the threshold.

"Hello there. You must be here for the wedding." A woman who appeared to be in her early fifties greeted them. She wore a casual, but neat, outfit of khaki pants and a plum sweater set. "My name is Olivia. I'm Max's assistant."

"She's my assistant, taskmaster, right-hand man and personal lifesaver."

Grace had seen Maxwell Hart's photo when she'd researched the vineyard's website. But he was much more handsome in person—tall and distinguished-looking with dark hair that was graying at the temples and a tanned face with deep smile lines. He removed his glasses and she was sure she saw a twinkle in his light blue eyes.

"Max Hart," he said, extending his hand to each of them in turn.

After introductions were made, they talked briefly about the specifics of the wedding ceremony and reception. The guest list was under one hundred. Max nodded as Grace explained the details and Olivia took notes.

"I have a couple ideas in mind for specific points around the site that might work best for you," Max said.

"We're just so happy that you're able to help," Emerson said. "Truly. Thank you so much."

"No problem. I'm happy to help. I feel horrible about the flooding that happened in the other section of the valley. A lot of those winemakers are good friends of ours. I hate to see them struggling. Plus, any friend of Xander's is okay by me. That boy really helped me out of a tough situation a few years ago. I owe him so much."

Interesting, Grace thought. She knew Xander handled Max's divorce. She couldn't miss the expression of gratitude in Max's eyes.

"Speaking of, where is Xander?" Max asked.

That's what she'd like to know. Once again, Grace checked her phone. He was now officially late.

"You'll probably want to hold everything inside this building, but I'd still like to give you a tour of the grounds and vineyard."

"That would be great," Grace said. "We can get some ideas for the photographs."

"Afterward, we've set up a lunch and wine tasting for you," Olivia said with a smile. "We want to make sure you like our product."

"That's so sweet." Grace beamed. "I can tell you right now that I already love your reds."

"Smart woman," Max said on a jovial laugh.

They continued to talk as Max showed them a large tasting room. There was a huge wooden bar and tables throughout the room. Floor-to-ceiling windows presented the deck and grounds beyond that. In the back of the building was a fabulous space that would work perfectly for the reception. It was a banquet room with an entire wall of doors that opened onto a brick patio. Lights had been strung across a pergola and Grace could envision how romantic and magical it would look at night.

"It gets cold out at night but we have space heaters and the firepits to keep everyone warm."

"This is so perfect," Emerson said dreamily, squeezing Jack's hand. Jack leaned down to place a soft kiss on her head.

Grace checked her phone again. Where the heck was Xander?

"I can't wait to see the rest of the grounds," Jack said.

Grace couldn't miss the excitement on his face. Emerson also seemed to be eager to go on the tour. She bit her lip and considered.

"Listen, why don't you guys start the tour and I'll wait for Xander."

"Are you sure?" But Emerson and Jack were already following Max toward the door.

"As soon as Xander shows up, just grab Olivia and she'll bring you out to us in the second Jeep. Her office is right through that door." Max pointed at a hallway full of doors.

"Sounds good."

Grace watched as her best friend walked off hand in hand with her fiancé. She couldn't help but feel a bit envious. To have a man look at her the way Jack gazed at Emerson, with love and a sense of…almost wonder at times… Funny how she could plan so many weddings, and be around so many happy couples, and usually she was able to keep that little green monster at bay.

But Emerson was so much more than the ordinary bride. She was her best friend. It was…personal. Seeing her this happy was forcing Grace to face the fact that she was lonely. More than that, she was ready for an epic, out-of-this-world, fairy-tale romance with a Prince Charming of her own.

An image of Xander flashed into her mind so forcefully she almost fell over. She wanted to snort. Xander may have saved this wedding, and he was definitely attractive. And okay, he could kiss like no one else she'd ever met. But he wasn't the type of man who could provide her with the happily-ever-after she so desperately craved.

Mainly because he didn't believe in the concept himself.

Just as she was about to check the time again, Xander came bounding up the front steps and practically threw open the doors. He was moving at record speed and he almost ran right into her.

"Whoa, slow down, cowboy."

"Grace. I'm so sorry I'm late. I got caught up in a deposition and then hit a traffic snarl on Sixty-six."

His hair was neatly combed and he was clean-shaven. The scent of his aftershave teased her senses on the afternoon breeze. He was wearing a tailored black suit that fit his body perfectly. Breaking up the formality was a purple tie and she thought she caught a glimpse of matching purple socks.

She held her hands up in front of her. "It's okay."

The expression of shock on his face was actually comical. "It is?"

She let out a huff of a laugh. "Yes. It's not the end of the world."

He rocked back on his heels and gave her a long once-over. "Every time I think I have you figured out, you do or say something to surprise me."

She waved away his praise with a flip of her hand. "I'm a wedding planner. The majority of my job is dealing with hitches and snafus."

His eyes roamed over her and then his face broke out into a smile. "You look really pretty."

She made a big show of glancing down at her outfit and running a hand over the top of her pant leg. "Oh, this thing? It's just one of my work outfits."

His eyes lingered a little longer and he wore an expression that said he knew exactly whom she had dressed for. Finally, he glanced around the foyer and down the hallway. "Where is everyone?"

"Max is giving Jack and Emerson a tour of the grounds. We're going to meet them. We just have to grab Olivia." Grace turned to the hallway and froze. She couldn't remember which door led to Olivia's office.

"Problem?" Xander asked.

"No… Yes. I can't remember where her office is."

They stepped into the hallway and Grace looked to the right and then left. "I think it's this one."

She rapped lightly on the door, then turned the knob and pushed it open. Xander was right on her heels. It only took a second to register that they were definitely not in Olivia's office. In fact, they were in what appeared to be a large storage closet. Then, Xander shut the door.

Plunged into darkness, Grace felt around the wall for a light until her finger came across a little switch. It wasn't very powerful, but at least she knew they were definitely in a storage room now.

"Oops," Xander said. He fiddled with the doorknob and then slowly turned around to face her. "It's, uh, locked."

"What?" She pushed by him and tried for herself. When the doorknob came off in her hand, she knew it was official. They were locked in the room.

Xander blew out a long breath. "What were you saying about glitches and snafus?"

Well…damn.

Xander held his breath and waited for Grace to tear into him. After all, if he hadn't been late, they'd never have ended up in a locked storage closet.

Once again, she surprised him. Grace began laughing.

"I'm happy you see the humor in this," he said slowly.

She shook her head. "Is there anything else to do? What is it about the two of us? Whenever we're together things just seem to go wrong."

One thing that wasn't going wrong was the way she looked. Xander couldn't help but take in that outfit, which somehow managed to be both professional and sexy at the same time. It showed off her ample curves and his eye was drawn to the big pink bow at her waist. His fingers itched to pull at it. She was like a decadent present waiting for him to unwrap.

"Xander?"

"Huh?" The sound of her voice pulled him out of what could have been a pretty heady daydream.

"I asked if you were okay? Your face is a little flushed. Are you claustrophobic?"

"No, I'm not. Sorry, long morning."

He took a moment to familiarize himself with the setting. There were extra tables and chairs piled up, a ton of boxes against one wall, shelves with supplies against the other. An old desk that had definitely seen better days was right in the middle of the closet. Grace put her large tote bag on it.

"I'll search for more light and you call Emerson. If she's with Max, then he'll know what to do. Or you can call the winery's main number to get Olivia."

"Good idea," she said. She dug through her bag and pulled out her phone.

Xander found another light in the form of a tiny lamp. But it gave off barely more illumination than a child's night-light. Still, he placed it in the middle of the desk. That's when he noticed that Grace was staring at her phone. She held it up above her head and then walked toward the door.

"I don't have service." She pressed on a couple of buttons, held the phone to her ear and then sighed. "Nothing. What about you?"

He pulled his phone from his pocket and went through the same production. "It's always been spotty up here," he said.

Her head dropped. "What are we going to do?"

"What people did before cell phones." He began banging on the door and shouting for help. After a few moments of that approach, he turned to face her. Grace was biting her lip and he could tell she was trying not to laugh.

"How'd that turn out for us?" she asked cheekily.

The door was thick, and silence engulfed them from the outside. "I'm guessing we're stuck in here."

She jumped up to sit on the desk. "Well, not forever. When Em, Jack and Max return, they'll see our cars in the parking lot and know we're here somewhere. We just have to wait them out."

He crossed his arms over his chest and eyed her. "I'm impressed with how you're handling this situation."

"Well, it's not my first time getting stuck in a storage closet."

"Really?" he asked.

She laughed. "Really. One of my first weddings at my last job was this swanky country-club affair. My boss sent me to the storage room to do an inventory on extra chairs for the cocktail hour. Next thing I knew, I was stuck and I didn't have my phone on me."

"What did you do?"

"I freaked out for a while. When that didn't help matters, I tried your trick of banging on the door. Eventually, a waiter heard me and let me out. My boss was none too pleased, as if the whole thing had been my fault." She laughed again. "Yet another reason to go into business for myself."

He leaned back against the door. "You're a good wedding planner, Grace."

Her cheeks turned an appealing pink color that matched her blouse. "That was nice of you to say."

He shrugged.

She glanced down at her hands and then back up at him. "Since we're alone, I wanted to…thank you."

He couldn't imagine what this was about. "For what?"

"For getting your friend to donate this beautiful space." She sighed. "You didn't see Emerson crying the other night."

*Thank God.* "I can handle a lot, but seeing someone I care about crying undoes me."

She nodded. "It was awful. But then you dropped everything and rushed over to help."

He shrugged and crossed the small space to join her on the desk. "It was no big deal."

She squeezed his hand. "Yes, it was, Xander. You really saved the day. And I can't thank you enough."

He didn't know what to say. He wasn't used to such sincerity from her. Instead, he changed the direction of the conversation. "What about you?"

"What about me?"

"Look at what you're doing."

"I'm the wedding planner and I'm the maid of honor."

"And you're the best friend."

A smile blossomed, lighting up her face with more power than the meager lamp could ever provide.

"You impress me, Grace." He leaned toward her.

"It must not take much to impress you."

"Don't do that. Don't downplay your talent." He paused. "You're not a princess."

She sighed in a very princess way. "Sadly, I am not."

He chuckled. "That's what I thought of you before. That you were some beautiful, optimistic princess with unrealistic expectations and no grasp on reality. Then I watched you with your clients and how you handled yourself at that party, and realized you are so much more."

Silence permeated the small space. Had he gone too far? Said too much? Overstepped his bounds?

She stayed quiet for a long time. Finally, she smiled and simply said, "Thank you."

Yet another surprise from her.

Her smile faded slightly. "If we're sharing confessions... I have to admit something to you. I always assumed you were just this hard-ass, insensitive guy. Seeing the way you made my best friend smile when she thought her wedding was ruined, well, it meant the world to me." She paused, collecting herself. "Maybe I was wrong about you, too."

He didn't know what to say. Her words, and the feelings behind them, shocked him.

"I mean, I know you hate weddings," she continued.

He rose, stretching for a moment. "Hey, I like weddings."

"What!"

"I mean, I think people spend way too much money throwing them. But overall, they're fun. Open bar, a little dancing, sometimes something fun like a photo booth."

"Photo booths are so fun. I always get excited when my bride wants one at the reception."

"You plan fun weddings, too?"

She peered at him. "Um, yes. I plan all kinds of weddings. What did you think I did?"

He shrugged again. "I don't know. I figured you for the fancy, black-tie weddings."

"I do whatever makes the couple happy."

"You like making people happy." It wasn't a question. But she nodded, anyway. "You care about people."

"I try to."

That was the caring, feeling, sensitive Grace Harris. But she was also independent, capable, intelligent and brave.

He looked into her eyes. Into the depths of those dark, mysterious eyes. She was drop-dead gorgeous. And each day that he spent more time with her she seemed to become even more beautiful. Both inside and out.

He couldn't stop himself. Not even if he tried. And he wasn't trying.

He reached for her hands and pulled her to her feet. "Thank you for what you said." He spoke softly.

"Back at you," she whispered. "I'm glad you see me differently."

He pulled her even closer. They stood almost nose-to-nose. "I think we both had the wrong impression."

She nodded. Her lips parted, drawing his attention there.

"First impressions aren't always right."

He pushed an errant strand of hair, which must have come loose from that sexy braid that ran across her head, behind her ear.

"Mine was," he said.

Confused eyes met his. "I thought you hated me."

"I kind of did." He gave in and ran a finger over that braid. Then he drew his hand down to cup her cheek, feeling her soft, silky skin. "But only because I was scared."

She brought her hands to his chest. At first, he thought she was going to push him away. But then she splayed her fingers across his pecs, as if making sure he was real and solid.

"You were scared of me?" she asked.

He leaned down to press a soft kiss at the edge of her mouth. She sucked in a breath. "I was scared of the reaction I had to you. I'd never seen a woman so together, so attractive, before."

She pushed her hands up to wind around his neck. "I was attracted to you, too." Her voice was barely louder than a murmur. But he caught each and every word.

"We finally agree on something."

"Xander?" she said.

He looked at the woman in his arms. He realized that he'd been fighting his attraction to her since the first second he ran into her. But when he allowed himself to be honest, he'd wanted her like this, in his arms, since that first moment.

"Yes?" he said.

"Just kiss me," she said breathlessly.

He wouldn't have been able to wait another moment. He pressed his lips to hers and everything felt right.

His arms came around her waist, drawing her even closer. Her lips were so soft, her body so warm. He wanted to lose himself in her.

She was making the most enticing little noises. He ran his hands up and down her back. Her fingers were tangling in his hair. She tilted her head and opened her mouth, inviting his tongue to mingle with hers.

This was the most intoxicating kiss of his life. He'd never felt so connected to someone. He wanted to stay like this, with her, forever.

They didn't stop until the sound of voices came from the hallway. They'd tilted their heads to the side, but their arms remained entwined around each other. Something had changed. Something significant. But Xander wasn't anywhere near ready to investigate its meaning.

Grace lifted a hand to cup his cheek. He couldn't read the expression on her face or the look in those eyes.

She nodded, as if agreeing with him about the enormity of what had just happened. It was also like she didn't want to talk about it. Not quite yet.

Slowly, they untangled, straightened their clothes and went to the door. They knocked against it until, finally, Max opened it and let them out.

## Chapter Nine

Grace spent the entire weekend working. There were so many details she was handling at once, that she was just waiting for the moment when her overcrowded brain would shut down. Or when her head would explode.

She'd moved from her office on the first floor to the upstairs living room and had an abundance of binders, lists and catalogs spread over the coffee table and floor, where she was sitting and multitasking. She was reviewing the seating chart for one wedding while texting with a different bride. She was trying to get the bride to climb back off the ledge after she'd gotten in a fight with one of her bridesmaids. She still had an addendum to a contract to go over, a meeting that was happening tomorrow morning to prep for and centerpieces to present to one bride so she could make her final decision.

Then there was the other thing. The thing she was trying desperately not to think about. The thing that was pervading every thought she had anyway, so her attempts at ignoring it were futile.

Xander.

She put her head in her hands and sighed deeply. What had that been between them the other day? She'd never been kissed like that in her entire life. Since she couldn't seem to concentrate on anything else, she closed her eyes and allowed herself to remember how it felt to have his lips on hers and his strong arms holding her tight. She shivered.

"Gracie!"

Her eyes flew open at the sound of Emerson's voice. "Uh, hey, what's up?"

All happiness and excited energy, Emerson plopped herself down on the couch and looked over Grace's mountain of work-related supplies. She frowned. "Still working?"

She knew Em felt incredibly guilty about adding to her workload. But she didn't want her best friend to agonize. She wanted her to enjoy her prewedding time, short as it was.

"Oh, it's nothing." Grace waved her phone. "One of my brides is having a meltdown. You know how it is. And I wanted to work on this seating chart up here, where I'm comfortable."

Emerson scrunched up her nose. She wasn't completely convinced. "Well, can I at least make you something to eat?"

"That would be great. Thank you."

Thirty minutes later, Grace and Emerson enjoyed grilled chicken, couscous and a salad, while Emerson helped her with the seating chart.

"See, if you just move these two guests over to table nine, then you can put the coworkers here and the two cousins who can't be at the same table will actually go in separate corners of the room. Perfect."

Grace shoveled the last bite of couscous in her mouth and studied Emerson's changes. "You're an angel. You have just saved my sanity."

"All in a day's work."

Emerson took Grace's empty plate into the kitchen while she cleaned up the mess in the living room. Then they reconvened to watch an episode of one of their favorite reality shows, *Say Yes to the Dress*.

"So it looks like the alterations on my dress will be ready in time," Emerson said during a commercial, beaming.

"Your mom has some killer connections. We owe her big-time."

"So-o-o…" Emerson began.

Grace glanced toward her and waited. Emerson wiggled her eyebrows. Grace asked, "What?"

"I spent most of the weekend with Jack, so you and I didn't get to talk about, you know."

Grace had no idea. They'd exhaustively discussed Hart of the Hills after their meeting via phone, text and email. Grace racked her brain but she couldn't remember any TV shows they'd wanted to watch. "What are you talking about, Em?"

Emerson was wearing her most innocent expression. "Well, I noticed on Friday when we were at the winery that your attitude toward Xander seemed to thaw."

Grace couldn't help but roll her eyes. Out of principle. "I don't know what you're talking about."

"You and Xander."

"Me and Xander nothing. He's still…"

"Yes?"

"He's, well, you know…"

"No." Emerson crossed her arms over her chest and waited. "Please tell me." Her eyebrows rose in anticipation.

"He's…" A great kisser. Hot as all get out. "He's stubborn," she finally responded, defiantly.

"So are you, Princess Grace. All I know is that when we got back from our tour and bailed you two out of the storage closet, something seemed different."

Grace turned to the TV and muted the bride with the unlimited budget, then faced her friend head-on. "What are you asking me, Em?"

"What exactly happened in that storage room?"

"Nothing." Wow, she hated lying. Especially since she was so bad at it.

"I don't believe you. I saw the two of you when you

emerged from the room." She fixed Grace with a calculating look. "There was something there."

"We were, um, talking about your couples' shower. That's all." Guilt washed over her.

Emerson sighed. "Actually, we're going to nix the shower."

"What? Why? You were so excited about it."

Emerson smiled, but it didn't reach her eyes. Grace knew she was trying to put on a brave face. "There just isn't time now. Jack already told Xander. It would have been fun, but there's no way we can do it now." She bit her lip. "Seriously, it's fine, Gracie."

Obviously, it wasn't fine. But Grace didn't want to push. She knew Em was right. There really wasn't time. Unless she wanted to give up sleep altogether. Or, have Xander plan the whole thing. She almost laughed at that. She could just see a hypnotist holding a tray of pigs in a blanket.

Something else occurred to her, and she really, really hated that it did. Not planning a shower with Xander meant she wouldn't get to spend that time with him. Funny how she went from dreading working with him to actually wanting to see him.

Grace unmuted the TV. She wanted to tell Em about what had gone down between her and Xander, but she wasn't sure herself.

A commercial for a local real-estate company came on the television. Grace decided to use it as her way out of this uncomfortable situation. She pointed at the TV.

"There is something we haven't discussed yet." Grace bit her lip as anxiety filled her. She really, really didn't want to have this conversation, either, and had been putting it off for far too long. But if she had to choose between discussing their living arrangement and her feelings for Xander, she was definitely going for the former.

Emerson sighed. "I know. The town house."

Emerson owned the town house where they lived and worked. Surely she wouldn't be staying there once she and Jack were married. As it was, she already spent half her nights at Jack's place, which was much better for a newlywed couple.

"You're going to sell, aren't you?"

Emerson sat back in her chair, indecision all over her face. "To be honest, I don't want to. I like working out of it. It's right in the heart of Old Town, close to so many of the vendors I use in my business."

"But…"

"But the mortgage is expensive."

"I can pay more," Grace said, desperation in her voice. "You haven't raised the rent since I moved in."

Emerson squeezed her hand. "And I'm not going to. Besides, I would have to double your rent in order to make my monthly payments."

"What if I paid rent?"

Grace and Emerson both turned toward the source of the statement. Amelia, Emerson's sister, stood at the top of the stairs, clasping her hands tightly together.

"Mia, what are you saying?" Emerson asked, using her nickname for her little sister.

Amelia sat down next to Grace. "I mean, I don't have a lot of references. I went from living at home to the sorority house and then back to Mom and Dad's before Charlie and I got married. Then, of course, back home again after Charlie and I separated." She looked down. "But I'm hoping you might still let me move in here."

Emerson's mouth fell open. "Are you serious?"

Amelia turned to Grace. "What do you say?"

Grace couldn't contain the smile. "Are you kidding? I would love to be roomies."

"Really? Seriously?" Amelia was beaming.

"Totally," Grace confirmed. "This is awesome. Now we

can continue working downstairs and Amelia can move into your room, Em."

Emerson hugged her sister. "Everything is working out so well."

Xander had been hearing about weddings all week. When he wasn't with Jack talking about his upcoming nuptials, he was hearing about Rachel, his recently engaged assistant, and her Pinterest page.

Then there was his newest client, Delilah Bagley, nee Richmond, soon to be Delilah Richmond again, if he did his job. Delilah, who has been married less than a year, found out that her husband cheated on her during their "amazing, lavish, fairy-tale" wedding with one of her bridesmaids. Pretty clichéd, in Xander's opinion. Interestingly, he'd heard more about this fairy-tale wedding than the actual marriage and relationship, but in any case, his client had a strong leg to stand on legally.

It was the end of the day and Xander walked Delilah out into the reception area. After their goodbyes, he turned to Rachel. "Anything else on the plate for today?"

Rachel was hardworking, organized and knew his schedule and to-do list better than he did. She glanced up from her laptop with a distracted expression. Completely unlike her.

"Sorry, boss, what was that?"

He sauntered over to her. "Anything left for us to do today or can we make an early night of it?"

Rachel offered him a blank stare.

"Rach?"

"Do you think I should have a tiered clause in the contract for my reception site?"

Ah, more wedding madness. He cringed on the inside, but tried to stay calm on the outside.

"Because I don't even know what that is, but I'm on this

really amazing wedding site called *Something True* and there are articles and even an entire chat room devoted to tiered clauses. Also, how many colors are too many to have as official wedding colors? I wanted to go with blue since that's both mine and Dre's favorite color. But should I have an accent color? Because this bride's Pinterest page talks about a main color and then three accent colors." She pointed at her computer screen.

Rachel's demeanor was serious. This was obviously important to her. For his part, Xander's pulse had picked up, and not in a good way. He took a step backward.

Contracts and clauses he could help with. Accent colors gave him hives.

"Did you see the Pinterest board I sent you?"

"You do realize I'm a guy, right? And I'm your boss."

This statement was met with zero remorse that she was clearly on social media during the workday. Honestly, Xander couldn't care less since Rachel always got her work done. Not to mention that he was probably way more intimidated by her than she would ever be of him.

"Also, I'm not on Pinterest," he told her for the hundredth time.

Rachel flung her head onto her desk. "I'm drowning here." She looked up again. "I'm swimming in a sea of tulle and centerpieces and engagement photos and wedding cakes. Help me!"

Xander smiled and sat down in the extra chair next to Rachel's desk. "It's going to be fine. I promise."

Rachel wasn't convinced. "How can you promise that?"

"Breathe," Xander instructed. "We're going to get through this."

"How?"

"I was going to get you something from your registry as a wedding gift. Since I like you and basically couldn't exist in this professional world without your assistance, I was thinking something good. Not your ordinary place setting."

"The KitchenAid mixer I'm going to register for?" Rachel's eyes practically sparkled at the suggestion.

Xander nodded emphatically. "Top-of-the-line. In any color you want."

"Best. Boss. Ever."

"However, I've changed my mind," he said. Rachel's smile faded. "Instead, I'm giving you the gift of sanity."

"Please don't say you're sending me to a mental institution. Although, a spa package would be warmly received."

"This is even better. Now, it's not wrapped, but I think that's okay. I am giving you the gift of a wedding planner."

Rachel froze and Xander counted the seconds passing in the completely silent room. Finally, she blinked—once, twice—before her eyes widened and filled with tears.

*Ughhh.* "Nope. Stop that. Don't do it." He jumped up and pointed at her face. "I can't take tears. Especially not from someone as strong and bossy as you."

"You're getting me a wedding planner?" Rachel stood, as well.

"I know a woman. She's pretty amazing."

*Amazing* was only the tip of the iceberg when describing Grace. He hadn't seen her since their trip to Hart of the Hills. Even though he'd been swamped at work, he'd found himself thinking about her more often than not. He wondered what she was up to and how the wedding planning was going. Multiple times he'd picked up his cell to text her but he wasn't sure they were on a texting basis yet.

"I—I don't know what to… Oh, my god." With that, Rachel wrapped him in the biggest hug. "Thank you, thank you, thank you."

After giving Rachel Grace's info and instructing her to have Grace bill him for everything, he sent his now happy and relieved assistant home. Xander then returned to his office, went through his emails a final time, gave a contract a final scan and closed everything down for the night. He waved goodbye to some of his colleagues still in their offices.

As he left, he meant to turn left and head toward his condo. Instead, he found himself veering to the right. There was no reason to walk in this direction. None at all. This path wouldn't take him home or to Jack's bar, where he often found himself after work.

But it would take him to Grace's house. He decided he was going that way because he should tell her about the arrangement he'd just made with Rachel. But deep down, he knew that wasn't the real reason. Obviously, since he could have simply called her.

As he walked up the steps to the front door of the town house she shared with Emerson, he actually saw her through the large picture window to the right. Her head was bent over her laptop and she was tapping a pen against lips that were painted a bright pink.

He checked his watch and realized that Grace's official office hours were over so he pressed the buzzer that was next to the door. Grace's voice came through the intercom.

"Hello?"

"Hey, Grace, it's, uh, Xander."

There was a long pause.

He leaned toward the window and waved at her. She was now standing behind her desk staring at him.

"Can I come in?" he asked.

"Oh, um, yeah, of course."

A loud buzz sounded and he opened the door. He entered a fancy-looking foyer decorated in tasteful gray and pink tones. A staircase led upstairs to the other levels. There were doors to the right and left, leading to Emerson's office on one side and Grace's on the other. A round pedestal table sat in the middle of the space with a large bouquet of fresh flowers on it. Their scent filled the space.

Grace was standing at her door. She wore a black dress with long sleeves and a necklace with bright pink stones that matched her lipstick. Her feet were bare and the sight of her in that sophisticated dress without shoes was insanely appealing.

Xander let his eyes roam from her toes up to her face. It was then that he noticed the dark circles under her eyes. Sure, she'd attempted to cover them with makeup, but when he peered closely he couldn't miss them.

"What are you doing here?" she asked. She stepped back so he could enter her office.

Another stylishly decorated room. He liked the crown molding and built-in bookshelves. But then he eyed the antique desk and two delicate-looking chairs in front of it that looked like a strong wind could blow them over. He opted to stand.

"Is everything okay?" she asked, worry causing a wrinkle to form in the middle of her forehead.

"Uh, yeah. I didn't mean to worry you. I was just…" What was he? Why was he here? "I was in the neighborhood."

"Oh." She leaned back against her desk. "You know, someone from your office called me ten minutes ago. Rachel Lemont."

"That was fast. I gave her your phone number just a little while ago. Allow me to apologize for any craziness, mass hysterics or crying."

Grace smiled kindly and all of those lines of stress and exhaustion melted away. "She was the typical bride. Nothing out of the ordinary."

He stared at her. Damn. This was what she dealt with on a daily basis? He recalled his conversation with Rachel from earlier and couldn't help but wince.

"Well, as her boss, I'm thrilled that you're able to take her on."

"Especially a boss who is paying the bill." She raised an eyebrow.

"She deserves it. She's an amazing employee. Plus, she put herself through school and I know she's still paying off her loans. Not to mention—"

"I think you're wonderful," Grace interrupted. Her face immediately blushed. "I mean, *it's* wonderful. What you're doing for her."

He shrugged. "No biggie. I'd be lost without her."

"Keep this up and pretty soon I'm going to think you actually like the institution of marriage." She narrowed her eyes playfully. "Or maybe you just want a job in the wedding industry."

"Busted."

She moved behind her desk and began shuffling papers around, replacing caps on pens, and then shut down her laptop. "What are you really doing here, Xander? Did Em send you?"

"No." He walked to one of the chairs and once again doubted its ability to hold his weight. He placed his hands on the back instead.

"Jack?"

"No," he repeated.

"So then… Why the visit?" she asked.

"First, I wanted to tell you about Rachel, but she beat me to it. Also, I came to check on you."

"Oh. Seriously?" She bit her lip.

He nodded. "I threw a three-week wedding at you. I had to make sure you weren't drowning."

She smiled and it lit up her whole face. "Ye of little faith. I'm fine."

"Grace?" he asked.

"I am *fine*."

He crossed his arms over his chest and hit her with a hard look.

"Okay, I'm a bit tired, but that's to be expected."

"How much sleep did you get last night?"

"I don't know. A couple hours."

Just as he thought. "How about the night before?"

She half laughed, half sighed. "Xander, I'm in the middle of three weddings. One happened over the weekend and thank God that's over. But I had to do all the postwedding work and I still have planning for my other two. It's not a big deal."

It was a big deal. She was taking care of the details for everyone else, but who was taking care of her?

He grabbed her hand. "Come on."

"Where are we going?"

"You need to eat something. I bet you haven't done that in a while, either."

"You're being ridiculous. I ate at… Well, what time is it now?"

"Eight o'clock." He lifted an eyebrow in challenge.

"I ate at…" She concentrated, the line reforming on her forehead. "Honestly, I have no idea. But, Xander, I don't feel like going out to eat. All I really want to do is take off this dress."

That comment caused an image to slam into the forefront of his mind. A very wonderful image of a very naked Grace.

Then he noticed her sagging shoulders and tired eyes. He checked his libido. This so wasn't the time for that.

"Let's go upstairs," he said, gesturing for her to lead the way. "I'm going to order you dinner and you can change out of your dress. Although, it is a beautiful dress."

"Thank you."

He suspected that she didn't have the energy to argue

with him. They walked upstairs. He carried her large tote bag while pink high heels dangled from her fingers. When they reached the living room, Grace asked if he wanted anything to drink.

Xander shook his head. "I'll get it. You go change."

"Oh, okay, thanks. The glasses are in the cabinet next to the—"

"Don't worry." Xander smiled. "I can find my way around the kitchen. Are you hungry for anything specific?"

"Not really. Just hungry." As if emphasizing the point, Grace's stomach growled loudly.

"How does Thai sound?"

"Perfect. Please order me pad see ew with beef."

"You got it."

He watched her continue up to the third level. Then he pulled out his phone and searched his Uber Eats app, happy to see that his favorite Thai restaurant was listed. He ordered for Grace and got himself a spicy Thai basil chicken. Then he made himself comfortable in the kitchen. He saw a half-filled bottle of red wine from Hart of the Hills. He poured half a glass for her and a full glass for himself, as well as a large glass of water. Then he settled in the living room.

When Grace returned, she'd changed into yoga pants and an oversize cotton shirt. Her face had been scrubbed free of makeup, which made her look younger.

"Better?" he asked.

"Much. Is that for me?" She gestured to the wineglass. He nodded and she took a sip. "This might knock me out."

"That's why you only got half a glass. Here's some water."

She put some music on as they enjoyed their wine. The food didn't take long to arrive and they both attacked their orders.

"This is my absolute favorite," she said on a satiated sigh. "You didn't have to do this, but I'm glad you did. Thank you."

"You're welcome."

While they ate, they talked about movies and television shows, finding they actually watched a lot of the same things.

"I would have guessed you were more of a reality TV fan," Xander teased.

"Oh, I am. Give me some Real Housewives or Top Chef any day of the week. But I also happen to love anything with zombies."

"Postapocalyptic stuff is so fascinating," he said, leaning over to steal one of her noodles.

After they'd exhausted entertainment options, they both expressed their disappointment that Emerson and Jack had canceled their shower. Jack had called him the day after they'd visited the winery. Xander understood the reasoning, but he was surprised to find he'd actually been kind of sad about it. Maybe he was more of a wedding planner than he thought. Or, maybe he'd just been happy to get to spend time with Grace and get to know her more.

"I know it would have been a lot of work," Grace said.

"But it felt like they were really looking forward to it," Xander finished.

When it appeared that Grace was getting full because she'd slowed down, she sat back, took a sip of wine and pinned him with a stare.

He put down his chopsticks. "What?"

"I'm wondering about you. We've established you do like weddings."

"Ye-e-s." He wasn't sure where this was going. "I don't like when people spend more than a down payment on them, but I generally enjoy myself at the party."

She curled her legs underneath her and leaned one arm on the back of the couch. "So it's really marriage that you don't like."

He took one last bite of chicken and then joined her on

the couch. "I didn't grow up with a very positive example of marriage. Most of my friends' parents were divorced."

She didn't say anything. Just waited patiently.

He didn't know what it was about her, but something had him spilling his guts. "Strangely, my parents were the ones who didn't get divorced."

"Why do I get the feeling that bothered you?" she asked, with a questioning look in her eyes.

"They have a horrible marriage," Xander said on a long exhale. "There hasn't been a day that's gone by when they didn't fight."

"A lot of couples fight."

He shook his head. He wished they fought like normal couples. "Not the way my parents do. They play dirty and nasty. They use anything at their convenience. Any weakness they can detect. They even use…me."

"Use you?" She looked alarmed. "How?"

"However they can. They cheat and then flaunt their affairs in the other's face."

"That must have been really hard to be around."

"It was. On the surface, we had everything. Everything." His voice grew raspy. "We had all of this money and nice things. Their house here in Virginia is immaculate. They have a beach house in the Hamptons and one down in Florida. We could go anywhere in the world. My childhood should have been ideal."

She reached over and twined her fingers with his.

"I had so much more than other kids and I felt ungrateful."

"Material objects don't make people happy," she said wisely. "They never have and they never will. Not long-term, anyway."

"Our holidays could have been, and should have been, something out of a Martha Stewart magazine. Instead, they were filled with shouting and accusations. They just…never got along. One of the most memorable times was when my father threw a huge platter of spaghetti into some historic mirror, shattering the glass and leaving a trail of marinara sauce on the wall in the formal dining room."

She blew out a long breath, her eyes growing wide and unbelieving. "Wow."

"Yeah."

"Why did they stay together all this time? For appearances?"

He ran a hand over his face. "I have no idea. It's never made any sense."

"Is this why you became an attorney?"

"I had always wanted to go into law. It was fascinating to me." He grinned at her. "Plus, I'm good at arguing my point."

She smiled. "I can attest to that."

"I picked divorce and family law because of my parents. It's not that I like seeing people separate. It's that I know from personal experience that those breaks are sometimes needed. Not only for the two people involved."

"For their kids, too," she said, nodding her head slowly.

He realized she was finally understanding. He didn't know why, but that made him extremely happy.

"So do you think I'm some spoiled brat?" he asked.

"Totally." She laughed and squeezed his fingers. "No, of course not. I think you had a tough childhood. I think you're trying to make it right by your choice in professions. And I think you're incredibly brave."

Brave? His head snapped up at that comment. No one had ever called him that before. Why would they? Wasn't he a poor little rich kid?

He wasn't even sure what Grace had been through in her life. All he knew so far was that it hadn't been idyllic if she was so tight-lipped about her parents, and her grandparents had raised her. Maybe he should ask her about her upbringing. Maybe he —

His thoughts were cut off when Grace scooted closer to him. Very close. He could feel her breath on his face. She pulled their joined hands up to her mouth and kissed his knuckles. One by one. With her other hand, she pushed back a lock of hair from his forehead and twisted it around her finger. Then those deep, dark eyes met his and he was gone.

She leaned into him and pressed her sweet lips against his. She cupped his face, with her hands on either cheek, and deepened the kiss, pouring herself into it.

Then she pulled away slightly.

"What was that for?"

"It was for that scared, lost little boy."

He touched a finger to her swollen lips, ran his thumb over the bottom lip. They parted for him.

"I'm not a little boy anymore." His voice was husky and his heart was beating at a million miles an hour.

"Then you need another kiss."

With that, she kissed him again. He heard a rough, primal sound. It may have come from him. He didn't know. How could he when her intoxicating scent was swirling around him and clouding his thoughts.

She pushed him back, his head hitting the throw pillows in the corner of the couch. Before he could do anything, she was straddling him. Not very princess-like, but sexy as hell.

She ran her hands over his chest, her touch eliciting a shiver. He reached up to her. Cupping her head, he pulled her mouth back to his. She came willingly and her hungry mouth sought his with more passion than he'd ever known.

He moved his lips to her throat. Her skin was so silky. She giggled.

"Sorry, ticklish," she said breathily.

Good to know. He'd remember that spot.

Then he couldn't remember anything when she slid her hands under his shirt. Suddenly, it went from slow and lazy to fast and fiery. Hands were everywhere, clothing was being undone. He didn't know why, but Xander desperately wanted her under him. With some tricky maneuvering, he was able to flip their positions on the couch.

His thigh was resting between her legs. Her eyes had darkened with lust. She was the sexiest thing he'd ever seen.

Suddenly, "The Imperial March" from Star Wars broke the silence.

"What is that?" Grace asked with a small laugh.

"Work." Xander pulled his phone out of his pocket and held it up.

"Equating your work with the evil Galactic Empire. Not sure what that says."

He was impressed she knew what the song was from. "You know Star Wars? I'm shocked. There are no singing animals or magic pumpkins." He untangled himself from her and rose.

"But there is a princess." She winked at him.

He laughed. "Be right back. I have to take this."

He answered the call with a gruff voice as he walked into the next room. But he had a heck of a time concentrating on his boss's words. All he could think about was Grace.

His intention in coming over here tonight had not been to make out with her, or to reveal the woes of his childhood. It had been… Well, he wasn't sure exactly. More often than not, he found his thoughts veering her way.

Ten minutes later, he ended the call and walked back into the living room. He stopped in his tracks at the sight of Grace, fast asleep on the couch. Her dark hair was fanned out over the pillows and her lips were formed into an adorable and appealing little *O*. She looked every bit the picture of a damsel waiting for her Prince Charming to wake her with a kiss.

He laughed silently and continued to watch her. He knew she needed the sleep but he was having a hell of a time stopping himself from leaning down and waking her. He wanted to gather her in his arms. Continue their earlier make-out session.

Xander wasn't sure how long he stood there. Never in his life had he simply watched a woman sleep. There was something soothing about being with Grace—even in this moment.

Finally, he grabbed a soft blanket that had been flung over the back of an oversize chair. He covered Grace, tucking the blanket around her shoulders, and allowed himself a moment to linger. He ran the back of his hand over her check. At his touch, she mumbled something in her sleep and the sweet sound packed a punch to his gut like nothing before.

Leaving her to rest, Xander took the dishes from their dinner to the kitchen. He loaded the dishwasher and put the leftovers in the fridge before he went back to the living room and tidied up the space as best he could. Grace hadn't so much as moved. Xander couldn't imagine how tired she was.

He scribbled a quick note and left it on the coffee table so she would see it when she woke up. Hopefully, that wouldn't be until the morning. With a last, longing glance at her, he turned off the lights and made his way downstairs and out the door, making sure to check that the door was locked behind him.

The door was locked, but suddenly it felt like his heart wasn't. For the first time in his whole life, Xander knew he was letting someone in. The strange part was that rather than feeling afraid, he actually felt at peace.

## Chapter Ten

"Interesting."

Grace looked up from her computer to see Emerson standing in the doorway holding a piece of paper. Grace had been ensconced in reviewing details of the catering contract for Emerson's wedding.

"What's interesting?" she asked absentmindedly.

"Ahem." Emerson gave a very dramatic show of clearing her throat before reading. "'Princess Grace, I didn't want to wake you.'"

Grace popped up. "Hey, give me that."

"Uh-uh." Emerson evaded Grace's attempt to snatch the paper. "'Thank you for an amazing evening.' An amazing evening with Xander Ryan. Really? Do tell, Gracie. Or should I say, Princess Gracie."

"Shut up." She once again tried to grab the note but Emerson dodged and continued walking around Grace's office.

She'd meant to put Xander's note in her bedroom. Right between the pages of her journal. Who knew why, but it charmed her that he'd left a note at all. She certainly hadn't meant to fall asleep on the couch. When she woke in the early hours of the morning to find herself wrapped in a blanket, the lights off and the space cleaned up, she couldn't believe that Xander had gone to such trouble.

Of course, the fact that he'd stopped by at all—and only to check on her—spoke volumes. Unfortunately, no matter how hard she listened, she wasn't sure what, exactly, those volumes were saying.

Emerson continued to watch her with an expectant expression. "Well? What happened? I leave you alone for one night…"

Grace folded herself into one of the chairs in front of her desk. Emerson joined her in the second chair.

"Xander came over."

Emerson waved the letter in front of Grace's face. "Ah, yeah. I figured that much out already."

Grace laughed. "Fine. We talked for a little bit. Oh, he recommended me to his office assistant. Then he ordered us dinner."

Emerson leaned forward. "And dessert…"

"Was homemade."

"I guess we're not hating Xander anymore, huh?" Emerson asked.

Grace sighed loudly. "I don't even know how it started really. But next thing I knew, we were horizontal on the couch."

"Yep, definitely not enemies." Wiggling her eyebrows, Emerson clapped her hands together. "Then what happened?"

"He got a call from work that he had to take. I guess while he was on the call I fell asleep. When I woke up this morning, he'd covered me with a blanket and cleaned up everything."

"Seriously?"

"Yeah. That's sweet, right?"

"Well, yeah. And kind of surprising for Xander. He doesn't seem the type to take care of a woman. Not that he isn't kind," Emerson hurriedly added. "What does this all mean?"

"I don't know."

"Are you and Xander a thing now?"

"I don't know," Grace repeated. "No. We aren't. Right?"

"If you don't know, I definitely don't, either."

"I'm not sure if it's a blessing or a curse, but to be totally honest, at the moment, I don't have the time to figure it out."

Right on cue, her phone rang. Saved by the wedding bell.

While Grace spoke to one of her vendors, Emerson left the room, returning moments later with two bottles of water. She handed one to Grace just as Grace ended the phone call.

"Are you sure you can handle all this?" Emerson blurted. "Don't lie to me, Grace. I'm really worried that you have too much on your plate."

Grace smiled at her best friend. Truthfully, she was exhausted. She'd executed one of her biggest weddings yet, a three-hundred-person, six-figure extravaganza at the Army Navy Country Club over the weekend. The only reason she'd even been asked to plan it was because the bride, Leann Tristan, had been one of her sorority sisters in college.

As far as weddings went, there were no major catastrophes. Only the small snafus that she'd come to expect.

But all of the last-minute late hours had cost Grace. She'd already been running on little to no sleep. There simply weren't enough hours in the day, and too much to do for the small wedding this weekend. Then it was right on to Em's wedding.

"Grace Harris." Emerson practically stomped her foot in frustration, interrupting her train of thought. "Tell me how you're doing. I'm a concerned BFF right now."

"There's no need for concern. I'm fine."

"Is there anything I can help with?"

Emerson had helped her plenty of times in the past, just as Grace had helped with some of Emerson's larger events. While Grace really could use the help, unfortunately, Emerson currently had her hands full.

"With what free time?" Grace asked honestly. "You're as busy as I am."

Emerson's face fell. "I am." She let out a loud, long sigh.

"Did we take on too much? Should we postpone the wedding and look for another space that would give us more time to prepare?"

When all was said and done, Grace was going to use this wedding as the event to which all other weddings she planned would be compared. She couldn't believe how much they'd accomplished already. Of course, there had been concessions, like the emailed invitations rather than the beautiful antique-quality invitations Mrs. Dewitt had found.

Leaning back in her chair, she said, "No. I know it seems tough now and we're both tired and anxious. But that winery is perfect. It's everything you've always wanted."

Emerson started pulling at her auburn curls. "But you're working so hard."

"This is my job." She reached for Emerson's hand and steadied it. "Even if it weren't my job, I would do this for you. I would do anything for you."

Finally, Emerson appeared to relax. "So I'm not running you into the ground?"

"The truth? Of course I'm tired. I have one wedding this weekend and then it will be your turn to be the princess."

Emerson's smile widened and her eyes twinkled. "Well, then. Let's gets back to you and Xander."

Grace groaned. "You are relentless. There is no me and Xander."

Emerson picked up Xander's note from Grace's desk and waved it around. "I beg to differ."

Grace tapped a finger against her lips as she considered. "Okay, we've definitely had a couple of…moments," she decided. "But so what? That doesn't mean anything."

Emerson tilted her head. She studied Grace for several seconds, until Grace began to fidget under her gaze.

"You're making me nervous."

Emerson leaned forward. "What are you afraid of, Grace?"

She didn't know what she thought Emerson was going to say, but it certainly wasn't that. "Afraid? What are you talking about?"

"I know you. You love romance. I'm no expert, but you're being stubborn about Xander. Something is holding you back. What is it?"

Grace opened and closed her mouth. She wiped her palms on her pants.

She didn't want to, but Grace couldn't stop the thoughts of her mother from infiltrating her mind. Of course, remembering her mother brought her right back to her meager beginnings.

Grace liked who she was now, despite her childhood. She was proud of how far she'd come. Still…she always wondered if she'd find someone who would also like who she was.

Who she truly was.

Grace pushed down the emotions that were bubbling toward the surface. She had to take a few fortifying breaths to keep the tears at bay.

Her mother hadn't wanted her. Why would anyone else?

Even though she told Emerson almost everything, she could never get herself to talk about her mother. So, she did what she always did. Made up a less emotional reason.

"Xander's not right for me, Em."

"What makes you say that?" Emerson held up a hand. "And don't say it's because he's a divorce attorney and you're a wedding planner. That's a cop-out."

"We're opposites in so many ways."

"And in others, you have so much in common. Jack and I both see it. So what's going on?" She lightly tapped a finger to Grace's head and then to her heart. "In here."

Grace sat back in her chair. "I want a real romance, a real happily-ever-after. Like you and Jack."

Emerson huffed out a breath. "Um, I wouldn't equate me and Jack to a fairy tale. We pretended to be dating for a month. I'd hardly call that ideal."

"But it all worked out in the end."

Emerson shook her head. "And it can work out in the end for you, too. I don't understand why you don't see that."

"Not with Xander. He doesn't believe in marriage." She considered explaining his parents' situation to Emerson, but instinctively held back. Xander hadn't said it was private, but she didn't feel comfortable sharing the personal information he'd shared with her in such an intimate moment. "I'm not even sure he has faith in relationships. I hold love above everything else. Love ends in marriage."

For most people. For herself, she wasn't so sure. How would she ever find someone to accept all of her?

She wanted that more than anything in the world. But, she just didn't know if she was good enough.

For now, she'd stick to planning the celebrations of other peoples' love. That would be enough. It had to be.

"Gracie—"

"I don't care if I'm being picky. I won't settle for less than I deserve."

Emerson's face softened. "I don't want you to settle. At the same time, I don't want you to wait around for some perfect man. No such person exists. Besides, perfection can grow very boring. Sometimes the most perfect things are actually imperfect, and that's what makes them wonderful."

Grace got what Emerson was hinting at. She thought Grace was being too rigid. And maybe she was.

At that moment, both of their phones pinged. A text came in for Emerson and Grace got a call from her next bride.

"Enough worrying, because we definitely don't have time for it." Grace waved her phone in the air.

Emerson grinned. "Back to work."

Back to work indeed. No need to worry about the distant future when she was too busy trying to be perfect for the next week and a half.

On Sunday evening, Grace sat outside at the top of the steps that led to her town house. It was windy, but pleasant. Clouds had dominated the sky most of the day. She leaned back and closed her eyes as a refreshing breeze swirled around her. Someone was already using their fireplace; the aroma of burning wood was a favorite of hers.

She'd considered bringing a glass of wine out with her, but she'd feared a few sips of alcohol would push her over the edge into sleep land, a place her body was desperately craving. She'd finished working another wedding the night before, and the adrenaline was finally fading.

The event had gone off without a hitch. At least, no hitches that the bride or groom had been aware of, and that's what mattered.

Her phone started playing "When You Wish Upon a Star," making her smile. "Hi, Grammy."

"Hi, sweetie pie. How did the wedding go?"

She filled in Grammy on the weekend.

"Sounds like everything went well. Another wedding down. One more to go," Grammy said in her cheery voice.

"Yes, but this wedding is Emerson's. Everything has to be perfect. I would never forgive myself if anything went wrong."

Grammy chuckled, her laugh warming Grace. "You say that about every wedding. Think of it this way—after Emerson's wedding, you will get a much-needed break."

"True. But—"

"No *but*s," Grammy said stubbornly. "Think positive. Think about what you're going to do when you are done and have some time off."

Grammy always saw the bright side of life. Grace indulged by closing her eyes and imagining a nice relaxing bath with her favorite lavender bubble bath. She'd follow that up with an early night in bed with a romance novel by her favorite author.

"Are you relaxing yet?" Grammy said in a soothing voice.

Grace smiled. "I'm thinking about it."

"Then my work here is done."

"But—but, Grammy." Grace worried her lip. She didn't want to verbalize what was really bothering her. The thing that was constantly on her mind: Xander Ryan.

"What is it, sweetie pie?"

Grace considered, but she wasn't ready to tell Grammy about Xander just yet.

"I'm really anxious. It's just six very short days until Em's big day."

"That's not surprising. It's a huge wedding that you've planned in an incredibly short period of time."

"I'm organized, and I go over all the details every day. But what if I've missed something? I'm bound to have forgotten something."

"Can you bring on some help? Just for this week?"

Grace had already thought of that. She leaned her head back against the house, closed her eyes again and sighed. "I've contacted three of the people I've used as temps before, but they're all busy. Bringing someone new on would just add to my stress."

"All I can tell you is that you are strong and capable. Even as a child, you were the most organized ten-year-old. Remember how you were always asked to be on the planning committees for proms and dances in high school?"

"I know. But, Grammy—"

"And who was it that always put together the events for her sorority? Even during that blizzard when you had to change everything at the very last minute."

"Me, but—"

"Trust me," Grammy continued. "You got this."

Grace smiled at her Grammy's faith in her. When she started going down those deep holes of thinking about her mom, it was Grammy who pulled her back out. "I love you."

Grace opened her eyes and almost jumped out of her skin. Standing at the bottom of the steps, his intense gaze trained on her, was Xander.

She wondered how much he'd heard of her conversation. By the way he was watching her—with concern in his eyes—she had a feeling he'd at least heard about her stresses.

"Uh, Grammy, I have to go."

Grammy reiterated her confidence in Grace and they ended the call. Staying seated, Grace turned her attention to Xander.

"What are you doing here?"

"I like to go for walks on Sunday nights. Clear my head and think about the upcoming week."

Something about that surprised Grace. She imagined him spending his Sunday nights differently. Maybe taking out some model or attending a party like the one they'd met up at only several short weeks ago.

"How's your grandma?" he asked.

"Good." She waited for him to ask about her, to bring up the stress he'd no doubt heard her mention to Grammy.

Instead, Xander rocked back on his heels, hands in his pockets, looking incredibly handsome. "Want to walk with me?"

Again, he threw her off balance. "Walk?"

"It's this thing that requires the use of your legs."

She rolled her eyes playfully. "I guess I can handle that. Give me one sec." She dashed inside to grab her keys. Okay, she may have also stopped by the mirror in the foyer to smooth her hair and make sure she didn't look too atrocious. Sadly, she could see the dark circles under her eyes and the pallor to her face.

Resigned to not looking her best, she locked the door and met Xander at the bottom of the steps. "Ready."

He grinned, and it took everything inside her not to go weak at the knees. He was so damn attractive.

"Where are we heading?" she asked.

"I'm going to buy you an ice-cream cone."

Again, not what she'd been expecting. "Ice cream?"

"Yes. See, ice cream is a dairy product that's been frozen and—"

"Ha. Don't you just have all the answers to the world's greatest mysteries."

"I'm very resourceful. Come on." He steered them toward King Street.

They walked in relative silence for a few minutes. Grace enjoyed the walk. The usual city sounds still surrounded them, but she knew that most people were inside their houses, preparing for the week ahead. Kids getting ready for school, worried about the homework they hadn't begun yet. Adults getting ready for the workweek. People watching football. The Redskins had the Sunday night game. Surely, people were getting their football food spreads ready.

Grace felt something brush her hand. She glanced down in time to see Xander interlace their fingers.

"You're holding my hand," she said, feeling stupid.

"I'm starting to worry about you," he said. "I know you just finished another wedding, but you really seem to be stating the obvious here."

She hip-bumped him. "I am pretty out of it," she admitted.

As they walked along the streets of Old Town, he began rubbing his thumb over her hand, eliciting a small shiver from her. She angled her body and eyed him. Xander offered her a cocky grin. If she wasn't so surprised that he was playing with her hand, she would have been annoyed at his confidence. Instead, she found him charming.

When was the last time a man held her hand? It was such a simple gesture, yet the way her body responded was nothing short of complicated. To her, hand-holding spoke more of developed relationships than easy flirtation. Xander didn't do relationships. Yet, he seemed so comfortable with their hands joined. And it felt right. Real and special.

It didn't take long to reach the ice-cream parlor. She was happy to see Xander went to one of the mom-and-pop places over a chain. She always tried to support the local businesses.

The place was empty, and they were greeted by two teenage employees. Xander ordered butter pecan in a cone and she went with straight chocolate. He paid, and they left the store, heading toward the water. They found a bench overlooking the Potomac and settled in to enjoy their cones.

The sun was almost finished setting over the river, but the clouds were doing their best to hide the usual colors of the straggling sun. Still, there was a dreamlike quality to the evening.

Boats were docked in the harbor. Aromas of cooked fish and other food emanated from the nearby restaurants. She looked to the right at the Woodrow Wilson drawbridge. Traffic was zipping across it as one of the water taxis that transported people between Old Town and National Harbor made its way underneath.

A loud cheer sounded from the closest restaurant. Grace and Xander turned to see a small wedding. The bride and groom were sealing the deal with a kiss as their guests applauded and whistled.

Grace couldn't stop her grin. She just loved seeing people happy. The wedding planner in her drank in the details of the ceremony. She'd guess about thirty guests. There was a small two-layer cake decorated in white and orange with an adorable cake topper. The flowers were tasteful, showcasing autumn colors. The displays weren't overwhelming. There was just enough to make the space special.

Only because this was her profession, she noticed the wedding planner, dressed in black, quietly moving on the edges of the room. She was lighting candles at the tables and fussing with the centerpieces.

"That's going to be me on Wednesday," she said to Xander.

"What's happening Wednesday?" Xander asked. He took the last bite of his ice-cream cone and wiped his mouth with a napkin.

"I'm heading out to Hart of the Hills early Wednesday morning. I'll check into the hotel where everyone is going to stay and set up as much as I can before Em and Jack get there on Thursday afternoon."

"Seems like extra special treatment," Xander said.

"Well, I have an extra special bride." Grace laughed.

They lapsed into a comfortable silence again. After Grace finished her cone, Xander took her hand again. Fireworks went off in her system.

"You know," Xander began. "I'm due for some vacation time at work. Why don't I join you on Wednesday?"

Grace's heart stopped and all the air whooshed out of her body at the mere suggestion of being alone in a hotel with Xander. "Join me?"

"Yeah. Do you have any help coming on Wednesday?"

She didn't answer, wondering if he'd overheard her tell Grammy she didn't have any help. He squeezed her hand.

"No," she said. "My subs aren't showing up until Friday morning."

"I'll make arrangements first thing tomorrow morning."

Xander and her alone for almost two days. Was that really a good idea?

"You really don't have to do that, Xander. After all, this is my job."

"Think of me as your assistant," Xander said. "I'll even let you boss me around." He winked at her.

Because she didn't want to appear ungrateful, Grace was left with no recourse but to relent. "Fine, come on up on Wednesday. But be prepared to work."

"Yes, ma'am."

Without warning, he framed her face in his hands and gently—so, so gently—kissed her. If they weren't sitting on a bench, she would have surely melted into the ground.

When he pulled back, he offered her an appealing grin. Then he grabbed her hand again and they began to walk toward her house.

They didn't mention the kiss or the fact that they were going to be alone together in a hotel. But that's all Grace could think about.

Xander said he would come prepared to work. The problem was that she had no idea how to prepare to be alone with Xander.

## Chapter Eleven

Anyone who said that wedding planners didn't work hard was seriously delusional. Or they'd never followed Grace Harris around for a day.

Xander and Grace had arrived at the hotel at nine in the morning. Their rooms weren't ready, but that didn't deter Grace. She had a list longer than the Potomac River, and immediately jumped into it.

They met with her contact at the hotel, ensured the wedding room block, toured the space, made sure the room they were using for the rehearsal dinner was adequate and reviewed the menu. While Grace and the hotel manager went through something called a BEO—whatever that was— Xander took a little time to familiarize himself with the hotel.

It was rustically decorated with fireplaces, leather couches in the lobby, stone accent walls and hardwood floors. But he noticed that it seemed to also have every modern amenity available: pool, fitness center, a large business center with a wall of computers and even an app. Plus, the views of the mountains were killer.

By noon, Xander would have paid big money for a nap. Grace had other ideas. He got the feeling if he even so much as mentioned a break, he would be staring down the wrong end of a wedding bouquet.

At the same time, he could tell she was losing fuel. Probably because she needed food. While she worked out some hitch with the transportation company that would be shuttling guests back and forth between the hotel and the winery, Xander made his way to a restaurant that was situated right behind the lobby.

He chose a table next to a large picture window so they would have a view of those majestic mountains. Then he ordered two lunch buffets. He'd have to be a little sneaky to get Grace in here, so he sent her a text claiming there was an emergency in the restaurant. Devious, but necessary.

He had to stifle a laugh when she power walked into the room, phone at her ear, clutching an iPad portfolio notebook. When she spotted him enjoying coffee at the table, her eyes narrowed and she slowed her gait as she made her way across the room to him.

She ended her call right as she reached the table. "What's the emergency?"

"You haven't eaten."

She sighed. "That's not an emergency. That's a nonissue."

He leaned back in the chair. "I disagree. A hungry wedding planner is an unproductive wedding planner."

She lifted her eyebrows. "Do I look like I've been unproductive?"

What she looked was amazing in her fitted black pants and long black-and-white blouse, with her hair pulled back in a ponytail and minimal makeup. "You look like you're hungry. I took the liberty of ordering you the lunch buffet."

At that moment, a waitress came by with their plates. "Would you like something to drink, ma'am?"

Xander could tell Grace was weighing her displeasure with his trick versus her need for common politeness. Manners won out in the end.

"An iced tea with lemon would be great. Thank you."

She dropped her tablet on the table, tucked her phone into the back pocket of those fitted pants she was wearing and picked up a plate. "I just finished working out the shuttle schedule. I still need to call the florist back because they have all of the bouquets mixed up. Have you ever heard of a MOH carrying a larger bouquet than the bride?"

He didn't even know what an MOH was. "Um, nope?"

"I know, right. It's ridiculous. After I sort that out, we need to get over to the winery. What are you doing?"

He'd placed a hand on her back and was steering her toward the buffet. "We will get to all of that, but first you are eating."

"Hey, you said you would let me boss you around."

"Eat first, boss later."

She peered at him and looked to be about to say something. Then she turned to the buffet and her body softened. "It does smell good in here."

Finally, she was making sense. "Let's load up."

They filled their plates and made their way back to the table. Grace took a bite of her salad and seemed to sink into her seat. "Okay, maybe I needed this."

"Is that your way of saying thank-you?"

She shook her head. "No. This is." She rose and walked around the table to him. Then she leaned down and placed a chaste kiss on his cheek. "Thank you," she whispered.

But as she began to straighten, he couldn't resist. He reached for her, pulling her back down. Her ponytail cascaded over her shoulder, tickling his face. Then he pressed his lips to hers. The kiss wasn't long, but it was potent with possibilities and want.

"You're welcome," he replied.

She seemed dazed as she returned to her seat. He liked keeping her off balance. Especially since every time their lips met, he became more untethered himself.

They finished lunch and headed over to Hart of the Hills. Max and Olivia were thrilled to help out. The four of them came up with a plan to add extra twinkly lights, per Emerson's request. They organized the space for the ceremony and reviewed where everything would be situated for the reception.

Hours later, Xander found himself back at the hotel, taking direction from Grace as they organized goody bags for the guests that would be staying in the hotel. They were using a small conference room on the main floor.

When his phone rang, Xander checked the caller ID and inwardly groaned. His dad was calling and he was in no mood to hear the latest drama.

Preoccupied arranging the items for the goody bags, Grace said, "Why don't you take that while I finish setting up?"

He wanted to protest and tell her that he'd much rather let the call roll over to voice mail. Left with no other excuses, Xander stepped out into the hallway and answered the call. "Hey, Dad."

"Hi, son. Where ya been?"

"I'm out in Virginia wine country, helping prepare for Jack's wedding. It's this Saturday. Remember?"

"Got my invitation. I'll be there."

Xander paused as a sinking feeling took over. "And Mom? Will she be here, too?" *Please say no. Please say no.* Not having his parents around to argue with each other would be one less thing to worry about.

"She's coming, too." His father sighed. "She'll have to leave her latest boy toy for the day."

Xander didn't reply. At this point, he didn't know what there was to say.

"You know she's seeing someone who works in a coffee shop? Ridiculous."

It wasn't defending his mother that had him speaking

up. Rather, it was the hypocrisy over the entire situation between his parents.

"Aren't you spending time with a waitress up in Sag Harbor?"

His dad coughed. "What does that have to do with anything?"

Xander rubbed the back of his neck. "Mom's seeing a barista. You're seeing a waitress. Do I really need to explain more than that?"

"Maybe I wouldn't be seeing anyone if your mother remained faithful."

Xander ground his teeth together, a bad habit he thought he'd broken after law school. "Maybe Mom could say the same thing." He began pacing the hallway.

His dad let out a mirthless laugh. "Your mother and I have been married for over thirty years."

"Have any of those years been happy?" Xander stopped pacing. He hadn't meant to ask the question and was surprised that it had slipped out. Since it was in the open, he waited anxiously to hear the answer.

Unfortunately, his dad didn't address it. "What's gotten into you, Xander? This is our life. Your mother flaunts her conquests in front of me. At least I have the decency of discretion. Speaking of, here she comes now. Do you want to talk to her?"

"No." Xander clenched his fists and leaned back against the wall.

"Fine. We'll see you on Saturday, then."

"You'll be together?" Xander asked.

"Of course." His father said this like it was the most obvious thing in the world. But based on everything they'd just discussed, it shouldn't be obvious. The entire thing was absolutely ridiculous.

Xander ended the call and stared at his cell phone. He

felt a headache brewing, a typical response to dealing with his parents.

He didn't understand. Why in the hell did they stay together? If they were unhappy enough to cheat on each other and, for the most part, live separate lives, why not end this charade of a marriage?

Xander leaned his head back against the wall and closed his eyes. This was marriage. Unhappiness, betrayal, tricks and drama. This was what he spent his days fixing. No one should live like this.

He pushed off the wall. His mood had plummeted and he felt sullen and angst-filled. He needed to go for a run or push himself through an intense weight workout. But there was no time for that. Instead, he had to return to the conference room and stuff minibottles of wine and other froufrou crap into goody bags. Like anyone even cared about this stuff. It was completely unnecessary.

He pushed open the door and stalked into the room. Grace was humming along to music coming out of her phone. She looked up when he entered and smiled.

Her smile was killer. It was pure and sweet and trusting. For some reason, it was the last thing he wanted to see. Here she was smiling at him and humming music, her hair framing her perfect heart-shaped face.

Grace truly had no clue. She spent her life worrying about insipid details like personalized M&M'S and bows on the backs of covered dining chairs. She had no idea what real people went through.

Xander had seen photos from his parents' wedding. They'd had all the bells and whistles. Where did that get them? Separate bedrooms and miserable lives.

Grace's face fell. "Is everything okay?"

Xander crossed the room and picked up a tiny bag holding the M&M'S with Emerson's and Jack's initials. He dropped it back on the table and ignored her question and the concern on her face.

"You charge people tens of thousands of dollars for this stuff."

She laughed lightly. "Well, candy doesn't cost quite that much."

"I'm being serious." His voice came out harsh and her head snapped up.

Grace shrugged. "It's their choice. If the couple has the money and the desire, what's wrong with that?"

"It's frivolous, stupid crap." He held up a votive candle with the date of his friends' wedding embossed on it.

"Maybe to you. Some people like this stuff."

He opened his mouth to argue but she held up a hand.

"I never force an option on a bride. I work with them. If they want a Christmas-themed wedding, I make it happen. If they only have five thousand dollars for a budget, I stay within those parameters, and steer them away from superfluous expenses like releasing doves and extravagant seven-layer cakes. It's a collaborative process."

"Collaborative?"

"Yes, it means that we work to—"

"I know what it means."

Her eyes flicked down. She finished tying a bow and then set the bag to the side. He could see her taking a deep breath.

Her shoulders drooped. "I thought you and I were working together well today."

Xander gestured between them. "You and I are very different."

She nodded slowly. "We've established that. But we've come together to help our best friends. Should I remind you that I never asked for your help? You volunteered to come here with me."

He jutted out his chin. "That was a mistake. I should have left well enough alone."

The color drained out of her usually rosy cheeks. "Where is this coming from? I thought, well, I mean—"

"You thought any of this was important?" he said. "Why? Because you probably grew up in Cinderella's castle at Disney World. You have no idea what it's really like for people out there."

If fire could fill people's eyes, the room would be toasty warm. It was clear that his bad mood had upset her. But not anymore. Now, she was furious.

"Do you really think I grew up in some kind of fairy dreamland?"

He crossed his arms over his chest. "Yeah, pretty much." Somewhere, in the far recesses of his mind, an inner voice was calling for him to shut up. He was upset about his parents and bombarding Grace with all of the emotions he couldn't handle himself. It wasn't fair, yet he couldn't seem to stop. "I think you spend so much time in the clouds arranging wedding parties and bouquet tosses that you have no idea what happens in the real world. What happens after the honeymoon. When your precious couples come to me wanting a way out."

She stepped back and her hand flew to her cheek as if he'd slapped her.

Seeing her react like that snapped him out of his mean streak. "Grace…"

She vehemently shook her head. "I don't believe in happy endings because I want to, Xander. I believe in them because I have to."

She had started out whispering, but with each word her voice grew stronger and stronger.

"*My* childhood was full of angst and heartache and abandonment. I've had a couple of great relationships, but I've never gotten close to happily-ever-after. Maybe Em is engaged to Jack now, but she was left at the altar before she met him. And her sister is in the process of getting divorced after only six months of marriage."

Grace came around the table and pushed him. Hard. "So don't think for one second that I know nothing about divorces and relationships that go south. Trust me, I know plenty."

Xander felt like such an ass. He'd let his parents ruin his day, and then in turn, he'd ruined Grace's. It was unfair and it was cruel. Especially when they'd been so productive. Not to mention, they'd been getting along better than ever.

"I'm sorry, Grace. I really am. I had a bad conversation with my father just now and—and, I took it out on you."

"At least you have a father to fight with."

*Whoa.* What did that mean? "Where's your fa—"

"You know what?" She raised her hands and then dropped them. "I'm done here. I'm done with you." Her chin trembled. "I need a break."

With that, she fled the room. Xander stood there, dumbfounded. He ran a hand through his hair and replayed their conversation. Their fight, was more like it. The fight that he'd caused.

Angry with himself, he knew without a doubt that he needed to make this right. Without overthinking it, he set to stuffing the goody bags. Following Grace's very organized and detailed notes, he was able to add all of the items. It felt like it took hours and definitely would have been more fun to do together. But he'd wrecked that idea.

He may have ruined her mood and her day, but at least he was able to help with her workload. Wasn't that the reason he'd come with her in the first place?

When he finished up, he cleaned up the space and put all the bags in the boxes provided by the hotel. Then he dropped them off at the front desk, along with the list that detailed which guests should receive them.

Now, onto Grace. He needed to make this right. There was no way she would want to see him. But he resigned himself to breaking down the door if necessary.

Xander felt like a real heel. He'd been a jerk to her because he couldn't handle his own crap. He was determined to apologize. Grace didn't deserve his wrath. No one did.

He took the elevator to her floor, and made his way down the hallway. Taking a deep breath, he knocked on her door.

When she opened the door, he could see that her eyes were red and puffy, and that beautiful face was splotchy from her tears.

"I'm sorry, Grace. I'm so very sorry."

She let out a whimper and her lower lip trembled. "I don't want to talk to you."

"I know," he said reluctantly. "I don't blame you. I shouldn't have said any of that stuff to you."

She pinned him with a no-nonsense stare. "You meant it. All of it. I know you did. That's how you really see me."

He opened his mouth to negate her words. Only, she was right. Wasn't that how he saw her?

"You're right and I'm not proud of myself. But…I'd like to know the real you."

Her eyes filled with tears and he could see her fighting them.

"Hey, it's okay."

Xander would have never associated tears with Grace. But something told him he didn't know the real Grace Harris at all.

"I don't deserve it, but I'd like a chance to talk. Please," he added.

Silently she stepped back, allowing him into the room. Grace had a suite. There was a sitting area with a couch and two overstuffed chairs, a coffee table and desk. He could see through a doorway that led to the bedroom with a large king bed. Her suitcase had been placed on a stool at the end of the bed.

"Nice room," he said as he walked toward the balcony.

"Meeting-planner perk." She blew her nose. "Sorry for the tears. Or, the almost tears."

He crossed the room and took her hands "Grace, you have absolutely nothing to apologize for. I was out of line downstairs. I was, well, an insensitive idiot."

She smiled. "Yeah, you were kind of an idiot."

He tucked her hair behind her ear. "You don't have to be so happy about it."

She laughed and he led her to the two chairs in the sitting area. They made themselves comfortable.

"Do you want something to drink? Maybe we should order dinner."

"Sure, if that's what you want." Even though she nodded, she didn't look confident. But Xander guessed that she needed some time. He didn't blame her.

She ordered the salmon and he went with a burger. While they waited for their food, he filled her in on the goody bags.

"What do you mean you took care of them?" she asked.

"I followed your list. You are really organized. I thought my assistant was detail-oriented, but you could put her to shame."

She smiled, but it didn't last long. "Well, did you add the bottles of water?"

"Yep."

"Two for each person, right?"

"I told you. I followed your list."

She worried her lip. "What about the paper with the shuttle instructions? Because that's really—"

"Grace, the goody bags are, well, good. If it was on your list, I did it."

"I should go down and pack them up as soon as we eat. I need to bring them up to the lobby."

"Done."

She blinked.

He couldn't help but laugh. "Grace, I took care of it."

The food arrived then. They both dug in, but it didn't take Grace long to return to the goody bags.

"Why did you stuff all the bags?" she asked, putting her fork down.

Xander dropped the fry he was about to eat. "I came here to help you. I know you wanted to get those bags finished today."

She looked unconvinced.

"If I hadn't upset you, we would have powered through them."

"You were helping me," she said.

"Yes."

She nodded and returned to her food. The rest of the meal passed quickly. He kept the conversation light.

"I needed that," Grace said when she'd finished.

"Do you have anything pressing you need to do tonight?"

She consulted her iPad, her eyes scanning the page as her finger scrolled through her master list. "Not really. I got to most of what I wanted today. I could always start—"

He gently took the iPad out of her hands.

"What are you doing?"

"I think we need to talk."

"About?"

He spoke softly, kindly. "I'd really like to hear about you. You said some things downstairs, and I realized I was presumptuous."

She bit her lip. Her gaze traveled around the room, seem

ingly content to stop on every object but him. "Do you really want to hear about my childhood? I mean, it's not something I normally talk about."

"I'm not going to force you to discuss something painful, but I want you to know that I'd like to hear about you."

Finally, she locked eyes with him. She remained silent for a long time. Xander didn't think she was going to talk. Then she took a big breath and began.

"My mom was a wild child. According to my grandmother, she'd been stubborn and headstrong since birth. Both my grandparents worked multiple jobs when my mom was growing up and they blame themselves for not being around enough. For giving her too much freedom." She shrugged. "But I don't think it's their fault."

"Some people are born with an independent streak," he said.

"One day my mom and grandparents got into a huge fight. Apparently, that was nothing new. But this one must have been a doozy."

"What were they fighting about?"

"I'm not sure." Her eyebrows drew together. "I think drinking or smoking or running around with the wrong crowd. No doubt a boy was involved. She'd been boy-crazy from an early age. Who knows. In any case, she ran away from home. She was only sixteen."

"Where did she go?"

"The details are fuzzy from this point on. Grammy and Pops did everything they could to find her but they didn't have any luck. They're pretty sure she left Florida almost immediately. One of her friends said she'd been dating an older boy."

Grace fidgeted in her chair, readjusting until she found a more comfortable position. "I was born in West Virginia when my mom was eighteen. We know that much. I have the birth certificate to prove it."

"Grace, we don't have to talk about this anymore if you don't want to."

She offered him a shy half smile. "Actually, it's kind of nice to talk about it with someone. I rarely do."

It meant a lot to him that he could hear this story. That she could trust him enough to share it.

"There's no father listed on my birth certificate. When I was little, my mom told me a guy named Ed Crosby was my dad. He lived in the same trailer park as us. Sometimes he would take me for ice cream or buy me a Barbie for my birthday."

She removed her shoes, placing them gently to the side. "One night Ed and my mom got into this huge fight. I was supposed to be asleep, but, of course, their screaming woke me up. I heard everything even though I didn't quite understand it at the time. She told him that he wasn't my father. She'd been lying my whole life.

"I asked her about it the next morning. She said a man named Damion was my dad. He'd been traveling through town and she'd cheated on Ed. Again, I didn't really understand any of this at that age. I was only five."

Xander's heart went out to her. His parents may have treated each other pretty badly, but at least he knew who they were.

"About a year later, my mom was seeing yet another man. I guess her six-year-old was cramping her style. Sometimes this nice lady who lived next door would watch me, but she wasn't home. My mom sent me to the car."

He sucked in a breath. He couldn't help it. In his line of work, Xander had heard a lot of stories about horrible parents. But Grace wasn't a client. Grace was someone in his life. Someone he was starting to have very real feelings for.

"Yeah, it was bad. It was cold. Not the height of winter but still too cold to leave a child out in a car. Even with my sleeping bag and the other blankets she gave me.

"That neighbor came home and found me in the car and called the cops. I was taken away from my mom that night." Grace shrugged. "Not that she cared. She was probably relieved."

"What happened?" he asked gently.

"My grandparents were tracked down by Child Protective Services and they came up to West Virginia and got me."

He felt anger bubbling up. "Where the hell had they been all this time?"

She shook her head, a pained expression marring her gorgeous face. "They never knew I existed. Can you imagine that phone call? 'Hey, you have a granddaughter. Not only that, she's been mistreated by her mother. Do you want her?'" She pulled her knees to her chest and hugged herself. "I never saw my mom again. I still don't know who my dad is."

Xander didn't really know what to say or how to help her. He tried to focus on something he could do. "Do you want to find your father? I work with a couple of different PIs from time to time. One in particular is phenomenal at finding people."

She shook her head. "Thanks. I don't think I want to find him. It's not about knowing the actual man so much. It's more that I want to know about me."

"What do you mean?"

"You may not like your parents but at least you know who they are and where they come from. I feel like part of me is missing. Worse, I'll never find it. I have an entire side of my family tree that I don't know. Where do I get my green eyes from? I can roll my tongue, which is a genetic trait. I get it from my dad. And I'm a morning person. I know my mom never was. Is that something from my dad, or is it all me?"

He could feel her frustration building and he desperately wanted to help her. Xander always played his cards close to his chest. For once in his life, he spoke from the heart.

"We both had rough starts in life. But yours was worse. Much worse. You have every reason to be jaded and bitter. Yet, you're the most positive person I know."

"I've chosen to be that way, Xander."

"That's what's so amazing about you. You've managed to do what I've never been able to."

"What's that?" she asked.

"Forgive. Move on. Accept. Be positive."

"It's not as hard as you think."

He choked out a wary laugh. "Easy for you to say."

She laughed lightly. "Like so many things, the first step is the hardest. After that, it's a piece of cake. You need to do things that make you happy." She met him with those mysterious dark eyes. Her lips pursed. "What would make you happy right now, Xander?"

He didn't have to think about it. He knew from the bottom of his feet to the top of his head what would make him happy.

Grace.

He leaned into her, pausing only for the briefest of moments to make sure she would meet him. Grace nodded, ever so slightly.

Xander closed the gap between them. He pressed his mouth to hers, capturing her lips in a kiss so sweet and so real that he immediately felt a loosening in his stomach.

This was happy. His happy. Her.

## Chapter Twelve

Grace's head was swimming.

She'd done something rare today. She'd delved into her past and shared her most secret feelings. Yet, that wasn't what was causing the light-headed feeling. It was Xander's firm lips on hers.

She needed to get closer to him. She rose from the chair, tugging Xander so he would join her. When he did, he engulfed her in his strong arms. They never broke the kiss. She was clinging to him for dear life.

He was intoxicating. She cupped his face in her hands, pulling him even closer. She tilted her head and opened her lips, and he took advantage by pushing his tongue into her mouth.

This didn't make any sense. If nothing else, talking about her past served as a potent reminder of where she came from and, more important, what she wanted. She'd meant what she'd said to Xander. She believed in happy endings because she had to. Knowing the harder side of life only solidified that idea. Unfortunately, the man currently causing her toes to curl wasn't going to be able to fulfill her wishes and desires.

Yet…she wanted him. More than she'd wanted any man in a long time. Maybe ever. But this wasn't going to end the way she needed. That's why she should probably stop kissing him.

Instead, she poured even more of herself into the kiss.

Grace didn't realize it at first, but she was starting to tip-toe backward. She clenched the front of his sweater in her fingers, urging him to follow her. He broke their kiss.

"Where are we going?"

"To the bedroom."

He paused, meeting her eyes. "You've had a really... I mean, I don't want you to think... That is..."

"Xander, stop." She giggled and stepped toward him. She placed a hand on his chest, felt the strong muscles beneath his sweater. She trailed her hand down to his stomach, delighting when he sucked in a breath. "Let's go," she said in her most sultry voice.

His eyes had darkened and she could tell he wanted her. But Xander didn't move.

"What?" she asked, nervous now.

"You've had a rough day. I don't want to take advantage of you."

She would have laughed if it wasn't for the serious expression on his face. The entire situation was comical. Here she was, completely aware that he was the wrong man for her, and she was urging him to give in.

She lifted his sweater, then let her fingers graze along the skin right above his waistband. He shivered. Raising onto her toes, she met his lust-filled gaze right before she bit his lower lip. Then she blew on the spot and pressed her lips to his. She used everything at her disposal. Her lips, her teeth, her fingers. She poured herself into the kiss even as her hands roamed his body.

Finally, he weakened. She felt him give in to her.

"Who's taking advantage of who?" she said.

He practically growled as he crushed his mouth to hers. His hands fisted in her hair and she loved the possessiveness that came over him.

When he bent over and lifted her in his arms, she let out a gasp. She knew she could be so easily swept away by him...

Her mind threw up a red flag, attempting to warn the rest of her body that as dreamy as the gesture was, Xander wasn't in this for the long haul. Best not to read too much into it. Unfortunately, her heart had no intention of listening to her head.

He arched an eyebrow. "You requested the bedroom?"

She nodded, trying to steady her breathing. "Uh, yeah."

Somehow he'd totally turned the tables. She'd started this, but he was now fully in control. He walked them into the bedroom, his eyes never leaving her face. Gently, almost reverently, he set her on the bed. Instead of joining her, he remained standing. He took his time taking her in, his eyes roaming from her feet all the way up to her head. He stared at her for so long that she started to fidget.

"Are you going to join me?"

"You're the most beautiful woman I've ever known. And one of the bravest. You deserve to be loved."

Grace was happy she wasn't standing because her knees would have definitely given out. She knew that Xander meant that her body deserved to be loved. It didn't matter though.

*You deserve to be loved.*

That was something she craved more than anything else. It was the phrase that she prayed she'd hear but was secretly terrified she never would.

She reached up and he accepted her hand. He came down to her and she loved the feel of his weight on top of her. They lined up perfectly. Her leg wrapped around his and she dragged her foot up his leg to tease him.

He'd moved his lips to the column of her neck. She shivered. He pushed back and offered her a wicked and totally sexy grin before returning to one of her most sensitive spots. His breath on her neck was driving her crazy. She felt her eyes roll back as she allowed herself a moment to simply enjoy every sensation.

When he began to nip and tug at her earlobe, Grace knew she needed to regain control. She reached for the bottom of his sweater, and in one swift movement, had it up and over his head. She tossed it to the floor. Then she gave him a shove, which clearly caught him off guard, and she was easily able to push him to his back.

Grace straddled Xander and offered him her cockiest grin. But her smile faded as she took him in. Who knew the stoic lawyer had such an amazing body? She planted her hands firmly on his chest.

"Wow." She couldn't keep the word from slipping out.

"Thanks," he said, amusement dancing in his eyes.

"I thought lawyers worked all the time." She ran her hands up and down his torso. His hard muscles were broken up by the sprinkling of dark hair that cascaded down his body and disappeared into his pants. "You work out."

"Not my favorite thing to do, if I'm being honest. Although, getting a reaction like this has me reconsidering. Maybe I'll increase my gym days." He reached for her shirt. "My turn. I'd like to see if wedding planners have time to work out."

She leaned back, out of his reach. "No. I'm not done with you."

"Aren't you bos—"

His words fell away as she began spreading kisses across his chest. As her tongue trailed down one side of his body and up the other, he shuddered. His hands fisted in her hair again. With a gentle pull, he brought her mouth back up to his and kissed the living daylights out of her.

She was panting from the intensity of the kiss when he reared up and switched their positions again. Somewhere along the line, he'd managed to get her out of her shirt. He was good. Damn good.

Now it was Xander's turn to ogle her. Normally, she'd have felt self-conscious. But there was no way she could feel anything but confident with the way his lust-filled gaze was traveling over her.

He reached behind her, and with a quick flick of his fingers her bra was loose. He slid the straps down her arms and grinned as he threw the lacy piece of fabric to the side.

"Lovely."

Then he went to work. He kissed and nipped at one breast and then the other. He fondled and caressed. She was writhing on the bed, biting her lip, as Xander brought her pleasure. When she didn't think she could take it any longer, she flipped them again.

"Hey," he said.

"Be quiet. I'm busy," she said with a wink.

She unbuttoned his pants, taking a moment to trail her fingers along the waistband. Xander groaned. Grace leaned down and pressed her mouth to his stomach. Then she replaced her fingertips with her lips and loved hearing his labored breaths.

Moving her hand lower, she cupped him over his pants. Xander bucked.

"Whoa, there," she said.

"You're killing me, Grace."

She laughed lightly and then freed him from his pants. Taking in his manhood, she had to pause and gather herself. *Oh, my.*

Xander took advantage of her breather to once again push her under him. At this point, they were lying horizontally across the bed.

Xander shifted, reached for his pants and fumbled around.

She realized what he was doing when she heard the foil packet.

When he returned to her, he took her hands, clasping them tightly in his own. He put them on either side of her head and looked deeply into her eyes.

"Ready?"

She nodded. "Oh, yes."

With that, he kissed her hard right before he pushed inside her. She moaned and clasped his hands tighter at the most personal of invasions. He paused, allowing her to acclimate to his size.

Xander leaned down and kissed her deeply. She met him with as much passion as she could muster. Then he began to move and, again, she kept up with him as best she could.

They found a sinfully intoxicating rhythm that had both of them gasping for air and calling each other's names. Finally, he released her hands and she held on to him for dear life as they fell over the edge together. As one.

Grace felt like she'd left her body. Her breath was still coming out in an uneven rhythm. Xander had collapsed on top of her and she could tell that he was as rocked as she was.

She ran her hands up and down his strong back as she tried to get her wits about her again. What they'd just done... had been beyond amazing.

"I'm crushing you," he said in a gruff voice that was sexy as anything.

He was, but she didn't care. In fact, she liked having him on top of her. She felt safe and content. She wrapped her arms around him tightly.

"Well, that's going to make it harder to get off of you."

"Exactly." She squeezed him tighter and liked hearing him laugh.

He angled his body so he could look down at her. Lightly,

he placed a kiss on her forehead. "You okay?" he asked softly.

"Oh, yeah. You?"

"Never better." This time, he kissed her lips. "Are you hungry? Thirsty? Cold?" he asked.

Grace had never felt more relaxed in her life. "I honestly don't think there's anything in the world I need at the moment," she said.

She snuggled into him. They were wrapped up in the soft bedsheets, lying on their sides, facing each other. The lights were low and she could hear rain hitting the windows of the room.

"I need to check the weather for Saturday," she said lazily. She should look it up on her phone, but her cell was far across the suite. She was too comfy to get up.

"You checked the weather about four hundred times today. I'm guessing it hasn't changed. It's not supposed to rain."

"And there's nothing we could do if it does rain besides enacting plan B. Still, it's stressful."

He pulled the comforter over her. "I repeat, are you hungry, thirsty? Need anything?"

"Are you taking care of me?"

He ran a hand down her arm, eliciting the most delightful sensation deep in her tummy.

"I'm trying to. You've had a rough day."

She cupped his cheek. "I've had rougher. I'm fine, Xander. Really. Well, actually, I am hungry."

"Ah, something I can help with. What are you in the mood for?"

She grinned. "Something chocolatey."

"Chocolate, huh?"

"You can never go wrong with chocolate. Besides, we need dessert."

He winked. "I thought we just had dessert."

She gave him a smacking kiss. "There's nothing better than a second dessert."

"Planning on staying here for a while?" He reached for the phone on the bedside table.

"Hopefully," she said, wiggling her eyebrows.

He placed an order with room service for two pieces of chocolate cake and a bottle of red wine. Then he returned his attention to her.

She trailed a finger along his jawline. He had the best face. Strong, distinctive bones and a square jaw.

"What are you thinking?" he asked.

"I think you should talk to your parents."

He propped himself up on one elbow. "Where did that come from?"

"I was thinking about my mom."

"We're lying here naked and you're thinking about your mother." He let out a gruff laugh. "I must be doing something wrong."

"Nothing wrong about *that*."

"And yet, you're thinking about your mom."

She mirrored his position. "It's just… I haven't seen my mom since I was taken away from her. My grandparents haven't, either. In fact, I have no idea where my mom is now."

"Do you want to talk to her or see her?"

"I don't know. But I don't even have the option. You do."

"Tru-u-ue." He drew the word out.

"My point is that you don't understand your parents. Their relationship doesn't make sense and it bothers you. There's a simple solution." She paused. Xander raised an eyebrow and waited. "Ask your parents what their deal is. Why are they staying together when they're clearly unhappy?"

He was quiet for a moment. "Do you think it will be that easy?"

"Pretty much. Even if you don't get the answer you want,

or think you want, at least you'll know. And then maybe you can start to put it all behind you."

He blew out a long breath. Then he leaned over and kissed her. "You're pretty smart, you know that?"

"I do. In fact, I know that we ordered the cake and wine less than five minutes ago and we have some time before it gets here."

He was already covering her body with his. "What should we do during that time?"

She laughed and pushed him so she was straddling him. "I have some ideas."

They spent the next thirty minutes going over some of those ideas in great detail.


The next morning, Xander woke up feeling good. He looked toward the window. The previous night's rain had cleared up. He heard birds chirping as sun streamed into the room.

He couldn't contain the grin as he thought about Grace. He'd been surprised when she'd initiated things last night. Surprised, but very, very happy. Xander couldn't deny that he'd wanted this since the moment he'd met her.

He rolled over, ready for more Grace. Only, her side of the bed was empty. He went up on his elbows and took in the room. She wasn't there. And the clothing they'd strewn throughout the room the night before had all been picked up and neatly folded. He grinned even wider. Figured she'd clean up.

He shuffled to the bathroom and was happy to find an extra toothbrush from the hotel. He saw that Grace had unpacked her toiletries. Bottles of perfume, lotion, and other female paraphernalia he didn't understand were scattered over the counter. He lifted a small glass bottle of perfume to his nose. He took a whiff and closed his eyes. Orange blossom. It was Grace.

When he was done in the bathroom, he made his way to the sitting area. The scent of coffee hit his nose before he'd rounded the corner. Once he stepped into the room, he found a room-service cart with a pot of coffee and covered plates. The distinct aroma of bacon wafted to him but his hunger took a back seat as he leaned against the doorjamb and watched Grace in action.

She had her phone to her ear and was scribbling away in her notebook. When she took a break from writing, she began organizing the creamer and little bowl of sugars that must have come with the coffee.

When she finished her phone call, she sat back and opened something on her phone. No doubt checking her weather app again.

"Morning," he called.

She jumped.

"Sorry," he said, crossing the room. He leaned over and kissed her. He'd meant for it be a quick peck but as soon as his lips touched hers, it went deeper. He cupped the back of her neck and she opened her mouth to him.

When they broke apart, she smiled. "Good morning to you, too."

"I didn't hear you get up."

"I didn't want to wake you. Coffee?"

"Sit. I'll get it. Want a refill?" He poured a cup for himself and then refilled her mug. He sat on the couch opposite her. "What time did you get up?"

She was studying her phone again. "Um, I'm not sure. I've been up for a couple hours."

He glanced at the clock on the wall. It was only seven thirty. Well aware that they'd been up and active until the wee hours, that meant Grace had barely had a couple hours of sleep. Still, she looked fresh and alert in gray leggings and an oversize pink jersey.

He tapped her notebook. "Any major problems?"

"Nothing life-altering. Just the normal hiccups. The alterations on Emerson's gown are coming down to the wire, but Mrs. Dewitt is dealing with that. Em's sister, Amelia, has been a huge help, too. She's really saving my butt. She's good at this stuff. In fact…" Grace sat back and tapped a pen against her lips. "I know someone with a start-up wedding website. I wonder if he needs any help. Mia would be perfect."

Xander wasn't sure if Grace was talking to him or thinking aloud. He rose and checked out the breakfast spread.

"I wasn't sure what you liked so I tried to get a little of everything."

*Little* was definitely not the word to describe the massive spread she'd ordered. Under the silver lids, Xander found a breakfast paradise of scrambled eggs, fried eggs, bacon, sausage, pancakes, French toast, regular toast, Danishes and oatmeal.

He arched an eyebrow. "Oatmeal?" He knew he sounded like a little kid but he'd never liked oatmeal.

She joined him and pecked his cheek. "That's for me. It's my favorite."

They filled up plates and ate together in the living area. Grace was fielding phone calls and emails, but still managed to carry on a conversation with him.

Xander couldn't help but think how hard she worked. It was coming down to the wire on a wedding she'd thrown together in three short weeks. She excelled at multitasking. As she entered something into her iPad, she was regaling him with funny stories of wedding mishaps and eating her oatmeal at the same time.

If he'd been in her position, he would be curled up on the floor in the fetal position.

"What are you thinking?" she asked, tilting her head. "You seem deep in thought."

He trailed a finger down the soft skin of her arm. "I was thinking about how many balls you have to juggle when planning a wedding."

Her phone rang. "Yet another thing involved with weddings, calls from the bride." She answered the phone. "Hey, Em. How was the conference? You wrapping up everything? Great. So I should see you in a couple hours." She listened intently for several moments. "Do not worry about anything," Grace said emphatically. "It's all taken care of. Your dress will be fine. I talked to the florist." Again, she paid attention to whatever Emerson was saying. "That is a shame, but there will be other times to wear it. In fact, why don't we go to dinner tonight. You can wear it then."

After Grace finished her conversation, she sat back, a pensive look on her face.

"What was that about?"

"The usual prewedding worries. Plus, Emerson was bummed about this really cute dress she bought for her couples' shower. Since we're not doing that now, I suggested she wear it tonight and we have dinner."

Xander felt bad. He was the one who'd booked their wedding to happen so soon. He may not understand it completely, but he did get that brides loved showers and all the wedding-related parties.

That's when it struck him. There was a way he could make it up to Jack and Emerson.

"I have an idea," he said, leaning toward Grace.

"What's that?"

"I was thinking about our first kiss."

He could tell that wasn't what she'd been expecting him

to say. She mirrored his pose, sitting forward and bestowing a chaste kiss on his lips. "In Jack's office at the bar."

"You were very mad at me," he said.

"That's because you were goading me. We were supposed to be planning Em and Jack's shower."

"Exactly."

"What?" she asked.

"We were planning a couples' shower for them. But then we had to scrap that."

She swept her arm out to encompass all the papers and notebooks on the table in front of them. "I do recall the order of events that brought us here."

"I feel bad. They didn't get their shower."

"Honestly, I don't think they mind. I know Emerson just wants to be married."

Xander sighed. "If it weren't for me, they would have gotten that shower."

Grace offered him an exasperated look. "If it weren't for you, we would still be searching for a new place to hold this wedding. You saved the day."

"I still feel crappy. Jack's my best friend and I love Emerson. I may not believe in marriage..." Grace froze at that statement. He couldn't miss it. "But they deserve every happiness. So I think we should throw them that shower."

"Okay...when? After the wedding? Because I had had this thought about doing something for them in about a month."

"No, before. Tonight." He was flying by the seat of his pants. But as soon as the words left his mouth, he knew he was onto something. "What do you think?"

"I love the idea," she said tentatively. "And while I try to be positive, even I don't know if I can pull a shower off in a few short hours. After all, guests are probably packing right now and will be driving up here soon."

He was an idiot. Hadn't he just been thinking how busy

she was and how she'd barely had any rest? Here he was giving her even more work to do. Grace was taking care of everyone else. But no one was taking care of her. Time to man up.

"I haven't gotten Em and Jack a wedding present yet. So how about I throw this shower?"

"Well…it's a nice idea, but do you know the first thing about throwing a couples' shower? At the last minute, to boot."

"Hey, I listened to everything you said back at Jack's bar."

A smile spread even as she shook her head. "I loved the ideas we came up with, but it's not likely they can be implemented today."

"What happened to your optimism?" He kissed her and stood.

"Where are you going?"

"To get dressed and get going. I'm going to do the best I can to make this an amazing night for Jack and Emerson. Be ready at seven."

"But, Xander—"

"Don't worry, Grace. I got this."

## Chapter Thirteen

Grace was shocked.

He'd pulled it off. Xander Ryan had actually managed to pull together a couples' shower at the eleventh hour.

Xander had figured out how to rent out the dining room of the hotel. They had the entire space for the whole night. With zero advance notice. It was unbelievable.

Grace spun in a circle. The room was decorated in tones of silver and gold, Emerson's wedding colors. He'd managed to find balloons, centerpieces, food and even a specialty cocktail called the Jack's Honey Bunny, which was a honey whiskey lemonade.

When she walked into the dining room promptly at seven o'clock, she'd found a fun party already in full swing. Music was playing softly in the background, people were mingling, food was being passed around by waiters.

She knew that Xander had been busy all day. She hadn't spotted him since he'd left her room earlier that morning. But she hadn't given it much thought because she'd spent most of the day at the winery. When Emerson arrived late that afternoon, they'd gone over everything she'd accomplished so far. Emerson had been in both bride and event-planner mode. A potent combination.

In all honesty, Grace had been anticipating a defeat in the couples' shower department. Glancing around the bustling room, she couldn't have been more wrong.

She sensed Xander before she saw him. Not only could

she smell his enticing musky aftershave, but something also seemed to change in the atmosphere when he was around. Something delicious and wonderful. She'd been so busy today that she hadn't had much time to think about their night together. But if she closed her eyes right now she could re-create every single moment in her mind. Every touch, every kiss, every second of pure bliss.

"What are you thinking about?" He'd come up behind her and whispered in her ear, his voice sending shivers of delight along her skin.

"Chris Pine," she lied.

Gently, he turned her to face him. "I think you're lying."

"Prove it," she said, tempting him.

"Gladly." With that, he kissed her deeply and passionately. Luckily, he was holding her or she would have slid to the ground in a puddle of glittery goo.

"You look amazing," he said.

She needed a little distance from him or she would climb up his body and have her way with him right there. So she stepped back and did a little turn. "You like?" she asked of the bright emerald dress she'd chosen. She ran her hand over it, loving the way the silky material clung to all of her curves and showcased her best assets. Her hair was pinned atop her head, allowing her long, dangly earrings to sparkle in the light.

"Very much," he said, his voice husky.

He didn't look bad himself. In fact, his dark suit and colorful tie fit him the best way possible, accentuating his broad shoulders and tall body. She couldn't wait to peel it off of him later. Or maybe tear. And throw across the room as they made their way to the bed.

As if sensing where her thoughts had run off to, he grinned. "You know where that green dress would look really good?"

She shook her head.

"On the floor of my room."

She pinned him with her sassiest stare. "I don't know if that's going to happen."

He stepped toward her. His eyes never left hers as he ran a hand slowly up her arm. Her breath caught as she tried not to show him how much he affected her.

"It's definitely happening." His confidence should have been off-putting. Instead, it was sexy as hell.

"Just because you got lucky with me one time doesn't mean—"

"It wasn't only one time…"

Grace could feel her face heating. She coughed, putting space between them once again. Luckily, a hotel employee interrupted them.

"Mr. Ryan, we wanted to let you know that the AV equipment is all set up. You are good to go with the slideshow."

"Great. Thank you so much, Henry. Start playing it on a loop when the bride and groom get here." He pulled up his sleeve and checked his watch. "Which should be very shortly. In fact, let's start dimming the lights."

"They're going to love this surprise." With that, the employee was gone.

Xander had not only thought of a slideshow, but also figured out how to implement one? Grace couldn't believe it.

"How? How?" She pointed at a framed picture of Jack and Emerson that hung on the wall. "How?"

Xander stuck out his chest. "I can't help it. I have mad wedding-planning skills." He flashed a mischievous grin. "Plus, I've learned that an American Express card goes a long way."

"Do I even want to know what this cost you?"

"Certainly more than the Instant Pot I was going to order

from their registry." He shrugged, as if everything he'd done was no big deal. "Jack is my best friend. He's worth it."

The lights flicked on and off a few times. People began to hush their conversations.

"Jack and Em are on their way."

"How did you get everyone here? The majority of these people weren't supposed to show up until tomorrow," she asked in a hushed tone.

"I had help from the hotel staff. We were all busy making calls. And since the hotel didn't have many reservations for tonight, they offered discounts on the rooms."

"You managed to contact all of these people, got them to drop what they were doing, pay for an extra night at the hotel—discount or not—and drive out here."

"I'm very persuasive." He winked, waited a beat, then he shrugged. "And let's just say that I owe Rachel even more than your wedding-planning expertise now. She really came through today."

"Hey, Xander, where should I put this gift?" one of Jack's employees asked.

Xander gestured to a large table set up at the back of the room. "The gift table is back there."

"Gifts? How did you manage to do that at the last minute?"

"Some people already had presents for the original shower. When I called people to invite them, I told them I would be making a run to the department store and asked if they would like me to pick up a gift. Several people took me up on it."

Grace couldn't help but be impressed. Xander had thought of everything.

"And the food? How in the world did they have time to prepare anything special?"

"That was definitely trickier. Again, the hotel really

helped me out. We have some stuff ordered in from local places and they filled in the rest with what they had on hand."

She watched him surveying the room, checking to make sure everything was set and where it should be. He faced her. His grin faltered. "Impressed?" he asked.

He was nervous. It was adorable. She offered her most reassuring smile. "You have no idea. I'm floored with what you did here," she said, a lump forming in her throat. "And I'm astonished with what you did last night." She held in a giggle at the blush that crept up his face. "But mostly, I'm awestruck with how wrong I've been about you."

"Grace—"

"They're right around the corner," Amelia called excitedly as she ran into the room.

She wondered what he'd been about to say. Secretly, she was glad he hadn't had a chance to finish because she'd shocked herself with her own words. She didn't know what caused her to say them. Although, she meant them. Every word.

When she'd first met him, she'd thought Xander was an uncaring, unfeeling, overconfident, workaholic playboy. He'd proven her wrong at every turn. He cared about his friends and his employees and colleagues. While he may be self-assured, his confidence had become endearing to her. She liked that he knew what he wanted and how to get it. Especially since one of the things he seemed to crave the most was her.

She felt her cheeks heating up just as Emerson and Jack entered the room. Grace loved a good surprise. She reached for Xander's hand as the happy couple walked into what they thought was an intimate dinner with Grace and Xander. Everyone yelled "surprise," held their drinks in the air and let out whoops and hoorays.

Emerson almost fell into Jack, who was busy looking from one person to another.

"What is this?" Em asked, her voice full of joy.

Grace put a hand to her heart. "She loves it. Oh, my god, check out how excited she is." She glanced up at Xander. "You did a really, really good thing here. Thank you." She went on tiptoe and gently pressed her lips to his.

"If it will help me get more kisses from you, I'll throw a shower every day."

"I hear we have you to thank for this little shindig." Jack was grinning from ear to ear as he and Emerson made their way over.

Emerson's gaze darted back and forth between Grace and Xander. She'd definitely caught their kiss. Grace avoided her questioning stare. She felt bad. She'd just spent the last three hours with her best friend and hadn't mentioned what had transpired between her and Xander.

Tentatively, Grace looked up and mouthed "later."

"Welcome to your surprise couples' shower," Xander said happily, oblivious to what was happening between the women.

Emerson hugged her. "Gracie, this is amazing. How did you do all of this?"

Grace shook her head and pointed to Xander. "It was all this guy's work. Most people buy place settings and ugly vases for wedding presents. He wanted to give you this."

Grace gave the couple room to lavish Xander with attention and praise. She liked seeing his face blush as Emerson planted a loud kiss on his cheek.

"Hey, where's the little mutt?" Xander asked.

"Cosmo is staying with Jack's neighbor for the next couple days," Emerson explained. "While we're on our honeymoon, my mom and dad are going to take on dog-sitting duties."

"Ah, man, I thought he would have looked great in a little doggy tuxedo walking down the aisle," Xander said.

"I don't know," Jack said. "A wedding and reception would have interrupted his ten-hour-long nap."

They all laughed. Then, Xander explained to Jack that they used Jack Daniel's Honey Whiskey in the Jack's Honey Bunny cocktail, and Emerson sidled up to Grace. "Well?" she asked.

Grace rocked back on her heels. "Well, what?"

"Gracie, don't give me that. I saw that kiss between you and Xander."

"We've kissed before. You know that."

Emerson shook her head. "That was different. I saw it. It was…intimate," she decided.

Grace was about to say that Emerson was imagining things, but she couldn't go through with it. She couldn't lie to her best friend. Especially not about something that was starting to feel very important.

Just then, Emerson's parents showed up. Grace squeezed Emerson's hand. "I'll tell you all the details later. I promise. Enjoy your party."

Seemingly appeased, Emerson smiled and hugged Grace. Then she and Jack began making their way around the room.

For the next several hours, everything went perfectly. Guests mingled and danced, food was served, Jack's Honey Bunnies were consumed. The guests enjoyed the slideshow Xander had put together. While Xander gave a toast to the happy couple, Grace helped with a slight problem in the kitchen. Other than that, there wasn't a hiccup to be found.

Grace had been considering hiring an assistant. Maybe she should get Xander's résumé.

"Thanks for helping out with the food," Xander said. He placed a hand on her lower back and steered her toward a free table.

They toasted with their cocktails as the music switched from a fast-paced oldie to a slow song. The dance floor filled up quickly.

"You don't happen to be looking for a new job in, say... event planning?" She batted her eyelashes at him.

Xander let out a hard laugh. "No way. No how. I'm glad everyone is enjoying themselves, but I honestly don't know how you do this on a daily basis. There isn't enough money on the planet to get me through that kind of anxiety."

She cocked her head. "What do you mean?" she asked, even though she was secretly pleased with his praise.

"This is some serious stress. I think I've gone through an entire container of antacids. No way my heart could take this kind of job."

"Seems to me that you have a very stressful job, too. I wouldn't be able to handle all that emotion."

He leaned closer. "Something tells me you would succeed at anything you put your mind to, Grace Harris."

She wasn't sure what to say to that. Instead, she swiveled in her chair. Xander followed suit. They watched Emerson and Jack dancing, their arms twined so tightly around each other that it was hard to tell where one of them began and the other ended. Grace didn't know when, but at some point, Xander's arm had come around her back. His fingers were lightly playing with the ends of her hair.

When she glanced up at him, Xander was intensely watching the couple on the dance floor.

"What are you thinking?" she asked. Part of her hadn't meant to ask that question out loud. But she couldn't contain her curiosity.

He nodded at Jack and Em. "That the two of them will have a long and happy marriage."

Good thing she was already seated because his words would have definitely knocked her over otherwise.

"What was that?" she asked.

"Jack and Em. They're made for each other. I can see them together for a long time." He faced her.

"No divorce?"

He shook his head.

"Xander Ryan, are you becoming a softy?"

He shrugged. "Maybe I'm starting to see things differently."

She couldn't believe what she was hearing. "Maybe I'm the most shocked girl on the planet."

He leaned toward her until his mouth was a hairbreadth from hers. "Maybe you're the reason I'm changing my mind."

Before she had time to swoon over his statement, his lips were on hers and that's all she could think of. Her hands came up to frame his face as his mouth devoured hers.

"Any more questions?" he asked, his voice sounding a bit strangled.

"Just one," she said coyly.

"What's that?"

"My room or yours?"

For the record, they went with Xander's room. But to be fair, he wouldn't have cared if they'd been in the hallway, a basement, a parking lot or under a table.

Unfortunately, it had taken them a while to escape the party. He supposed that was only fair since he was the host. Still, his brain had been on hiatus ever since she'd uttered those four little words.

*My room or yours?*

"When did this start?"

Xander almost jumped at the sound of Jack's voice. He'd been preoccupied watching Grace trying to say good-night to Emerson and her parents for the last twenty minutes.

The room had thinned out. A few stragglers remained on

the dance floor while some others were around one of the bars getting in their final drink orders.

"Huh?" he asked Jack.

"You and Grace. When did it start?"

Xander finally gave his best friend his full attention. "When did what start?"

Jack expelled an annoyed sound. "Don't give me that. You haven't taken your eyes off her since we got here."

"She's beautiful."

"Yes, she is," Jack agreed.

He agreed a little too quickly. Xander drew his eyebrows together. He knew Grace was gorgeous, but he wasn't sure how he felt about someone else saying it. Even Jack.

"And clearly you guys have stopped fighting long enough to realize that you have feelings for each other," Jack continued, oblivious.

Xander worked his jaw. He wanted to deny it. He spotted Grace across the room. She threw back her head and laughed. Her entire face lit up. He grinned.

"Yep, relationship city." Jack slapped him on the back.

"Whoa, whoa, whoa. Who said anything about a relationship?"

"Actually, you've said very little. I'm just filling in the blanks."

"Maybe you're wrong." Xander took a swig of water for his suddenly dry throat. "You ever think of that?"

Jack glanced over at Grace and then returned his attention to Xander. He shook his head. "Nope. I'm not. You guys are in deep."

*I sure am.*

Where in the hell had that thought come from? "I wouldn't go that far," he said, trying to convince himself more than Jack. "But we've…you know? That is, Grace and I have… Damn." He ran a hand through his hair.

Jack let out a loud chuckle. "I have never seen you tongue-tied over a woman. And how long have I known you?"

"Too long," Xander said dryly.

Jack looked like a little kid on Christmas morning. "This is great. You and Grace."

"Shh." Xander quickly glanced around the room, but there was no one nearby. "I don't know what Grace and I are right now, or even if we're anything. You know I don't do relationships."

"And you know I never planned to stay in Alexandria." Jack gestured toward his bride-to-be. "Things change."

Xander knew things changed. Didn't he see how much situations could transform on a daily basis at work? Wasn't work, coupled with his parents' insane situation, the reason he shied away from relationships?

And yet...didn't he want to go upstairs with Grace more than anything he'd ever wanted in his entire life?

It wasn't only for the sex, either. Maybe that was part of it. But it definitely wasn't the whole picture.

Grace caught his eye. She bit her lip, even as a smile was blossoming. Then she nodded her head at the exit.

"Gotta run. I have a hot date." He practically threw his water glass at Jack in his haste to leave. Then something made him stop. Something deep down inside of him. Part of the reason Xander loved practicing law was because he had great admiration for the truth. Even as a boy, he'd never been able to lie.

And the truth was that he could no longer imagine not being around Grace. It didn't make any rational sense. They hadn't known each other that long. They'd begun their acquaintance with constant bickering. Yet, out of all the people who'd been at the party—many of whom were close friends of his—he didn't want to be around anyone but Grace.

Moreover, he was already thinking about what would

happen after this weekend. He had a work event coming up on his calendar. Another boring gala. But with Grace by his side, the evening could actually be fun.

Not to mention that as the weather continued to cool down and the leaves took their final bows, the holidays would be right around the corner. Christmas in the nation's capital was so much fun. Maybe they could go to Mount Vernon or visit the White House Christmas tree.

What was he doing? Planning a future that featured Grace.

Xander waited for the panic to ensue. It didn't. In fact, the more he pondered it, the better he felt. Going through life with someone.

Xander took a deep breath. "I'm leaving now. I'm leaving with the woman…" He took a gulp. "I'm leaving with the woman I'm in a relationship with."

## Chapter Fourteen

Finally, Xander's wish came true and he was in his room. Grace had made a quick stop at her room to grab a few personal items.

While she slid out of her sexy heels, Xander went through the music on his phone until he found an appropriate playlist. A soft, slow melody filled the room. Grace looked up, surprise on her face.

He didn't respond. Instead, he simply scooped her up in his arms and began to move.

"What are you doing?"

She was off balance. Good. Join the club. Xander had been off balance since the moment he'd met her. From the second he'd laid eyes on her, it had all led up to this moment. All the fighting and bickering, flirting and teasing.

But here, where they were alone, with the moonlight streaming into the room and the music creating a romantic atmosphere, he could admit that he'd wanted her from the beginning.

"Xander?" she asked.

"I'm dancing with you," he said.

"I noticed that."

He brushed a light kiss over her forehead. "Do you not like to dance?"

"Oh, no. It's not that. I love to dance. It's just that I thought we would…" Her voice trailed off as her eyes drifted toward the bedroom.

Ah, she'd assumed they'd go right for bed. He thought back to the night before. He supposed he could have been more romantic. They'd gone from fighting to talking to making love. No romance involved.

She deserved more. And as shocking as it was, he realized that he wanted more, too. He wanted to enjoy being with her, and he wanted Grace to relax and revel in the night, too.

He spun her out and brought her back to him, enjoying her laugh and her flushed cheeks.

"You're a good dancer," she said.

"My mom made me learn. I complained every single second through the entire first lesson. But I have to admit that it's come in handy over the years."

"I bet you do this with all the girls."

She'd said it lightly, flippantly, but her expression quickly changed, as if her own words had sunk in. Xander got it. Grace still thought he was a playboy.

He shook his head as he turned her around the room. "No. Besides some formal work events and the occasional wedding, I reserve my dancing for special women."

She relaxed in his arms. Meeting his gaze, she grinned. "Are you saying I'm special?"

"Oh, yes." He wanted to say more but the words caught in his throat. Instead, he pressed his lips to hers. She tasted sweet, like the cocktail she'd been enjoying downstairs at the party.

The kiss went on for a long time. They stood together, swaying to the music, as their arms were wrapped around each other, their mouths fused together.

Finally, she broke away. With a hand to his chest, she said in a breathy voice, "I need a minute."

"Of course." If his erratic heartbeat had anything to say about it, he needed a minute himself.

Grace ran a finger over his bottom lip and then disappeared into the bathroom. Xander crossed the room to the window. He put his head against the cold glass. What was happening to him?

A knock on the door pulled him out of his thoughts. Who would be at his room at this hour?

He opened the door and found room service waiting.

"I'm sorry, I didn't order anything," he said.

"This is a gift," the attendant said and handed over an envelope. Then he pushed the cart, covered with a white tablecloth, into the room and left it right next to the door. He tipped his hat and quickly backed out of the room. Xander didn't even have time to tip the guy.

He ripped open the envelope and read the note. He strained not to roll his eyes.

Tell her it's from you. Thanks for the party. Enjoy!
—Jack

Xander lifted the domed silver lid and found chocolate-covered strawberries. There was also an ice bucket with a bottle of champagne chilling and two flutes.

He shook his head. He didn't know whether to strangle his friend or hug him. In any case, why let good champagne go to waste? He popped the cork and filled the flutes. For good measure, he turned the lights low.

Xander turned at the sound of the bathroom door opening, a champagne glass in each hand. Then he froze. He couldn't have moved for a million dollars.

Grace stood there, framed by the light from the bathroom, wearing lingerie in the same emerald-green color as her dress. It was all lace and silk and molded to every ample curve she had. She'd let her hair down and it was hanging in soft curls over her shoulders.

She ran a hand down her side while the other was propped

up against the door frame. She was every man's fantasy come true.

Xander had never seen anything more beautiful, more erotic, more amazing, than Grace standing there in her green lingerie.

"What's that?" she asked.

He had no idea what she was asking. He tried to speak but his mouth was dry.

Luckily, she answered for him as she crossed the room and took a glass of champagne from his hand. "Did you order this?" She ran a finger over a strawberry. "I love chocolate-covered strawberries."

Finally, his brain caught up to other parts of his body. He sipped his champagne, more to wet his throat than for the taste. "I'm supposed to tell you that it's from me." He offered her Jack's note.

"How sweet."

"It would have been sweeter if I'd thought of it myself."

She placed a hand on his cheek. "You've done so many amazing things today, Xander."

"Not for you."

"You made my best friend incredibly happy. That makes me happy."

"You deserve more."

She placed her glass on the table. Then she took his flute and also put it down. Moving closer, she wound her arms around his neck. His hands went very naturally to her waist. "When you say things like that to me, I get butterflies in my stomach."

"What about when I do things like this?" He kissed one eyelid, then the other. He couldn't resist placing a kiss on the tip of her perfect little nose. Then he brushed her nose with his, back and forth, before finally pressing his lips against hers.

He couldn't miss her intake of breath. She shuddered in his arms, which only caused him to tighten his grip.

Their mouths came together as one. He couldn't tell who wanted the other more. All Xander knew was that he'd waited far too long to get to this point.

They did a walk-dance into his bedroom. Their mouths stayed fused the whole time. Tumbling onto his bed, Grace let out a giggle as he covered her body with his.

He ran a hand along the sexy lingerie. "I like this. A lot."

"Good," she said with a triumphant grin.

"But it needs to go."

"That's good, too."

In one quick move, he had the skimpy material off her. She gasped and he took that as invitation to meld his lips to hers again. Her hands were moving frantically over him. She quickly undid the buttons on his shirt and hastily pushed it aside. She pressed her lips to his chest and he sucked in a breath.

They rolled over the bed, fighting with his belt and pants in a frenzy to get them both completely undressed. When they were finally naked and skin touched skin, Xander couldn't have said which end of the bed was up. All he knew was that Grace was beneath him, already panting, even as she reached down and cupped the area that craved her attention the most.

He reared back. There was something he needed to do first.

"What's wrong?" she asked, attempting to push herself onto her elbows.

He rooted through the nightstand until he found the con- 'om. "Nothing, don't worry."

Once he was prepared, he returned to her and that beauti- smile. Together they tumbled back onto the soft mattress. 'ander indulged by fisting his hands into all that thick dark hair. She kissed him soundly, wiggling beneath him as she tried to line up their bodies.

He entered her smoothly and slowly. Her intense stare met his and they never lost eye contact. Not the entire time they moved together. It was the most intimate moment of his life.

When they'd both fallen off the cliff, he gathered her into his arms. And held on tightly, held on for dear life.

Afterward, they lounged in bed, enjoying the strawberries and champagne. She was making him laugh as she told him stories from her time as an intern. It felt good to be so relaxed and at ease with someone.

The laughter turned to flirting and the flirting morphed into lust. Soon, they were entangled in each other's arms again and then made love a second time.

Later, Grace slept. Xander was wrapped around her, and he ran a hand over the silky smooth skin of her arm. Her breath was coming out in slow exhales and her body was completely relaxed.

He loved the way she felt all curled up into him. In fact, he couldn't remember feeling more content in his life. It had been a long day, from planning an entire party to actually attending the party and then to his extracurricular activities with Grace. Yet, he wasn't tired. Maybe because his mind was racing as he tried to figure out what was happening to him.

He didn't do relationships. He never had. But with Grace, he couldn't imagine not having her around. Now that he'd been with her, in every way possible, it was inconceivable to walk away.

Xander pressed a soft kiss to her temple as he considere The last thing he wanted to do was hurt her, but that w exactly what he was afraid of. He had issues and he kr it. Deep-rooted issues that stemmed from his parents. How could he bring that into Grace's life?

He recalled her words from last night. Maybe it was finally time to talk to one, or both, of his parents. Ask them why their relationship was the way it was. Maybe then he could get over whatever was stopping him from entering one-hundred-percent into a relationship with Grace.

She made a sweet little noise and snuggled even closer to him.

Because being without her was no longer an option.

Grace was having the most wonderful dream. Her body was being cherished by a fantastic man. A man who made her feel wanted and desired and... loved.

Sadly, the dream ended all too soon. She peeked through heavy eyelids and realized it was early in the morning. The sun was barely shining through the windows, reminding her they'd forgotten to close the curtains the night before. They'd been busy with, ahem, other activities.

Her mind came awake quickly. Much faster than the rest of her body, which was feeling heavy and sated. She knew she needed to get moving. It was the day before Emerson's wedding and there was a ton left to do. She visualized her many lists and began organizing the best way to proceed.

Then she rolled over and took in Xander's handsome face. She had to take just one moment. One second for herself. Xander was on his side, facing her. He was fast asleep, his breathing slow and heavy. She resisted the urge to run a hand over the sexy stubble on his face. Or to fix the hair falling onto his forehead. Not to mention wanting to lean over and press her lips to his. To wake him up properly.

Grace twisted to check out the time on the clock again. Nope, definitely no time for that.

With a very regretful sigh, she quietly slid from the bed.

That's when she realized she was completely naked. She ran a hand through her hair until it got stuck. Oh, boy, she couldn't wait to see what a mess she was.

Grace quickly collected her belongings and entered the bathroom.

"Yikes," she squeaked at her own appearance. Thank goodness Xander was fast asleep. He did not need to see the raccoon eyes courtesy of her eye makeup or the bird's nest on top of her head. Not to mention the red splotches on her face, no doubt from that sexy stubble.

She did her best to clean up with the limited toiletries she'd brought down. When she felt presentable enough to make a fast walk-of-shame back to her room, she turned off the bathroom light. With a last look at the sinful male, she almost caved and jumped back in bed. But with a sigh, she left the room.

When she reached her suite, she immediately threw a pod in the Keurig. A text message came through.

Hey, you left me.

Hey, you're supposed to be sleeping, she countered.

Hard to sleep without you snuggled up next to me.

Her heart skipped a beat. Grace leaned back against the wall with a hand to her chest and bit her lip.

When had this happened? When had Xander Ryan wormed his way into her life?

She looked down as another message came through to her phone.

I had a great time with you last night. I can't wait to s◀ you again.

If she thought her heart skipped a beat before, it was nothing compared to the humongous flip it just did. She couldn't wait to see him, either. And it wasn't just about the sex, although that was fantastic.

She liked talking to Xander. She liked the way he was confident but not cocky. She liked the way he looked at her, like she was the most beautiful woman on the planet. She really liked the way she felt when she was with him. Like everything was right in the world. Even in the middle of planning a very stressful wedding, he'd managed to soothe her nerves and keep her calm.

Grace did a little pirouette and then fixed her coffee. She needed to jump in the shower, dress and get the day started. But first, she crossed the room and leaned against the window. It was going to be a pretty fall day. The leaves were at that perfect state of changing colors but not yet falling. Birds were singing and the sky was a deep, clear blue.

She felt like she was in the middle of a fairy tale. Finally. Xander was making all her dreams come true. He was just perfect. When they were together, everything was perfect.

After all the years of angst and heartache, it was a strange feeling to be happy with how things were. She'd never gotten over the abandonment from her mom. That's why she wanted things to go on a certain way. With Xander, she had that chance.

And nothing could go wrong. She wouldn't allow it. Her fairy tale had to come true.

## Chapter Fifteen

"You realize you just poured syrup in your coffee and milk on your pancakes."

"Huh?" Xander looked up at Jack's statement.

Jack pointed at Xander's plate. Xander glanced down. "Oh, damn."

"What's with you? Enjoy those strawberries last night?"

Xander offered a finger of choice to his best friend, who only laughed. "The only thing I'm going to say is that Grace loved them, so thanks for that."

"I'm here for you. For example…" He gestured for the waitress to come over. "Could you please get my lovesick friend here a new plate and mug? Love has blinded him."

"How sweet." The waitress smiled and rushed to fulfill the request.

"I am not lovesick, you ass. I'm just tired."

Jack winked. "I'll bet."

Xander threw his napkin at him. "Not like that." Well, maybe a little. "I was busy planning a party all day yesterday for you."

Jack was enjoying every second of this. Since it was the day before his wedding, Xander decided to let him have his moment of triumph. Luckily, his cell rang, anyway.

"My dad." He waved the phone in front of Jack. "Be right back."

"Great. I'll try to get labels for the milk and syrup while you're gone."

Xander flicked his finger up again and walked out of the restaurant into the hallway.

"Hey, Dad."

"Hi, son." Alex Ryan's strong, loud voice bellowed through the phone. "I wanted to tell you that I had a client reschedule a meeting to this afternoon so I won't be able to make it there until tomorrow morning. Can you relay that information to Jack and Emerson?"

"No problem."

"I'm sorry I won't be able to attend the rehearsal dinner," he said.

"I don't think it's a big deal. But I'll let Jack and Em know, and Grace, too."

"Who's Grace?"

Jack started at the question. Who *was* Grace?

She was everything.

He leaned back against the wall in the hallway. "She's the wedding planner." Xander found it odd that he actually wanted to tell his dad about Grace. He held himself back, though. There was something else he needed to talk about first.

"Dad, I have to ask you a question."

"Uh-oh, this sounds serious."

"It kind of is." Xander was underplaying the importance of what he was about to ask. This was the question he'd had most of his life. He couldn't even begin to fathom what the answer would be.

"Let's hear it," his dad said.

He raked a hand through his hair. "Why have you and mom stayed together?" He paused, taking a big breath. "With all the fighting and cheating and insults, why have you never just gotten a divorce?" He sucked in a sharp breath. As much as he wanted to know the answer, he was terrified of hearing it.

"Ah, I wondered if you'd ever ask me that."

Really? He had? "And? What's the answer? Why have you stayed together?"

His father remained quiet for a very long moment. Finally, Xander heard him cough. "Because we didn't have a prenup."

Xander blinked. Then he waited. There had to be more to it.

"You're thinking there's more, right?" his father said, reading his mind. "I'm sorry to disappoint you, but that's the reason."

"You've put up with all of this angst and fighting and discord over a little money."

His dad sighed. Xander could see him now. He was surely in his home office, sitting behind the massive oak desk that had belonged to his grandfather. He would turn at some point and wander over to the large picture window that looked out over the gardens.

"We're not talking about a small sum of money," Alex continued. "I've informed you of all the assets, gone over our portfolio."

"Sure, but, Dad—"

"I don't care about the money I've made. But I do feel protective over my family's money. I know how hard my father, and his father, worked to build our business from the ground up. There was so much blood, sweat and tears that went into it."

Xander's mind was racing as he tried to process this very strange news. "Does Mom know…? I mean, did you ever discuss separating, er, is it really about the money?"

Despite everything, his dad laughed. "It's about a lifestyle." He sighed again, loudly. "I hate to admit this, but it's also about appearances. Your mother may not like me sometimes, but she does enjoy her lifestyle."

Xander wanted to punch the wall. This was absolutely ridiculous.

"Listen, Xan, your mother and I weren't always like this. We really got along in the beginning. I wouldn't have married her if it had been like this. She was fun and sweet and full of life. I couldn't wait to marry her."

"You married her because of me," Xander said softly. At least, that's what he'd always thought. He was born eight months after his parents' anniversary date.

"What?" He heard shock in his father's voice.

"Mom got pregnant and that's why you married her."

"Who told you that? It's nonsense."

Xander froze, quickly redoing the math in his head. "It is?"

"We got married because we were in love. Or we thought we were. Maybe we were in lust. We were definitely young. You were conceived on our honeymoon."

"But my birthday..."

"You were born a month earlier than your due date. Tiniest little thing I'd ever held."

Xander's mouth fell open. For most of his life, he'd assumed his parents married because of him. He'd hoped they hadn't stayed together because of him. In fact, he realized that was why he hadn't had this conversation earlier. He didn't want to be the reason for two people's ongoing unhappiness.

His dad went on. "We met as college students. Your mother was working in a restaurant that I used to frequent quite often." He chuckled. "I went there because she worked there, if you must know. The food was horrible. She was poor. Really poor."

"Did that bother you?"

"Not in the slightest. But it did irk your grandfather. He

liked your mom for the most part, but he was definitely of an older generation with very set and stringent ways."

Xander's grandfather had passed away when he was ten. They hadn't been superclose, but he had enjoyed the time he spent with Poppa Ryan. He'd spoiled Xander with toys. But he also used to talk about the value of a dollar and hard work.

"I'm surprised Poppa didn't make you sign a prenup."

"I'm sure he would have if your mother and I hadn't eloped."

His parents had eloped? How was it possible that Xander never knew this? "Wait a minute," he said suspiciously. "There's a wedding photo of the two of you hanging in the front sitting room."

"After we eloped, and your poppa yelled at me for a couple of days, he threw us the society wedding that was expected of someone in my position. Then we went on our honeymoon and eight months later, we had you."

"When did it start to go bad?"

His dad mumbled something under his breath. Xander waited.

"You know, Xan, it doesn't really matter." He exhaled loudly. "I know our marriage has affected you. I tried to ignore that fact over the years. I'm sorry about that because it hasn't been fair to you."

"You didn't answer my question about when things went bad."

"I'm not going to."

Xander knew that resolute tone. He'd heard it many times over the years. *Don't take the car out this weekend. Be home by eleven. Get an A in algebra or no summer camp.* There would be no talking his way out of it.

"It doesn't matter when things went downhill. It's between me and your mom. You need to stop worrying about us. Go out there and live your own life. Make your own mistakes."

Xander shook his head, feeling a massive headache beginning.

His dad reaffirmed that he would be at the wedding tomorrow and they ended the call.

Xander's mind was swimming with a million new things to obsess over. From his parents eloping to the fact that they didn't get married because of him. But the one thing that stood out was the prenup. At least, that's what Xander focused on. After all, he saw countless clients with the same issue. They postponed divorce due to a money issue.

He watched Emerson bounce into the restaurant with her sister in tow, reminding him of why he was here. His best friend was getting married.

Suddenly, he felt a renewed energy. Maybe he didn't find out everything about his parents today but at least he learned one thing. And it was something he could make sure Jack, his oldest friend, didn't have to worry about.

He whipped out his cell and punched the button for work. Rachel picked up on the first ring.

"Rach, I need you to do me a favor. I'm going to be putting together a quick file."

He couldn't save his parents' marriage, but he would make certain that he helped his best friend.


"What did you call me up here for? I was about to take a little pre–rehearsal dinner nap."

Jack sat down in one of the chairs in Xander's room, leaned back and crossed his legs at the ankles.

"Nap time can wait," Xander said. "I have something that is much more important."

Jack snorted. "According to my soon-to-be bride, nothing is more important than beauty sleep."

Xander rolled his eyes. "You're beautiful enough. Now

take a look at this." He presented him with the file he'd been working on for the last couple of hours.

Jack scanned the document, confusion showing on his face. "What is this?"

Xander sat in the chair opposite him. "Granted, it was rushed. But we can hash out the specific details and go through any assets and such."

"Is this...?" Jack glanced up, meeting Xander's eyes. "Is this a prenuptial agreement?"

"Yes."

"For me and Emerson?"

"You see anyone else getting married around here?" Xander said. Jack clearly needed that nap, and not just for beauty reasons. He wasn't making any sense.

Jack read through the prenup for another minute. Then he closed the folder and handed it back to Xander.

"What are you doing?" Xander asked.

Jack shook his head. "I don't need this."

Xander clutched the folder in his hands. "Dude, listen, you should really consider this."

"Seriously, I'm good. Emerson and I aren't doing a prenup. We've discussed it already."

"You have?"

Jack laughed lightly. "Don't you think if I was going to require any kind of legal document pertaining to my marriage I would have come to you?"

Xander placed the folder on the coffee table. He opened the cover and scanned over it again. Then he met his best friend's stare. "Yeah, I guess you're right." He gulped. "Listen, I just wanted to make sure you were covered."

"Ah, gee, I knew you cared." Jack slapped his leg. "I'm not mad. But I am curious. What made you think to do this?"

Xander rubbed at his temples. Then he told Jack all about his conversation with his father. When he was done, he fe spent. He ran a hand through his hair. "So I just thought that I would make sure you were never put in the same position as my mom and dad."

Jack nodded. "I get it. I do. But Em and I are not your parents. We're never going to be your parents," added quickly when Xander tried to protest. "And I have some more news that's going to blow your mind."

"Hit me," Xander said, tired, but mildly curious.

"You are not your parents, either."

"Thank God for that," Xander said dryly.

Jack's smile faded. "Listen, I know I've been giving you crap about this thing between you and Grace. But I'm actually really excited for you, and not just because it's Grace. I've seen what you've been through over the years. I'm happy that you've finally realized that you can be happy, too. Especially with a woman as hot as Grace."

Xander leaned forward and punched him in the shoulder. "Shut up." As he sat back, he frowned. "Can I be happy?"

He was truly asking. He thanked his lucky stars for Jack, because his best friend seemed to understand that he needed a real answer.

Jack's brow wrinkled as he narrowed his eyes. "It doesn't matter that your parents have a crazy relationship. It doesn't even matter if every couple on the planet showed up in your office wanting a divorce."

"What does matter then, Obi-Wan?"

Jack leaned closer and rapped his knuckles against Xander's chest. "What's in here. Your relationship with Grace is what's important and other people's relationships have no bearing on that."

Xander felt like someone had just dumped a bucket of cold water over him. He'd just woken up from a lifelong sleep that had kept him from relationships.

Jack was absolutely right. It didn't matter that his parents kept up their insane charade or that he dealt with crappy marriages on a daily basis. None of those things had anything to do with Grace.

Because when he closed his eyes and thought of her, he was filled with good feelings: positivity, hope, laughter... and love.

He was in love with Grace. *Holy crap!*

Xander waited for the fear. None came. He searched for dread, but only felt excitement.

He looked over at Jack. "I'm in love with Grace Harris."

Jack grinned. "Well, then. It's a good day."


It was a good day. Grace felt like her fairy tale was coming true and she couldn't believe it was due to Xander Ryan.

Plus, her best friend was about to marry the man of her dreams. Despite the short timeline, the wedding was on track with minimal issues.

Yes, everything was good today.

She practically strutted into the lobby of the hotel. She needed to swing by the restaurant and make sure everything was set for the rehearsal dinner.

"You look happy."

She stopped at the sound of Xander's voice, butterflies assaulting her stomach. "Hey, handsome."

"Back at you, gorgeous."

He was propped against the far wall, near the fireplace, looking every bit the *GQ* model. She would like nothing more than to ravish him right here and now. Instead, she would settle for the small kiss she laid on him. Even that sent sparks of electricity all through her body.

"What are you doing down here?" she asked, putting some space between them so she didn't follow through on the ravishing.

"Waiting for Jack. He's under the impression he's going

to hear my best man's speech. Little does he know I have no intention of sharing it."

"Ah. Are you going with funny or sentimental?" she asked.

"Both. It's going to be epic."

She laughed. "We'll see." His confidence was so damn appealing.

Her phone let out a little *chirp*. She read the text message and frowned.

"What's wrong?" he asked.

"Hmm? Oh, nothing. My phone is almost out of juice." She rifled around in her large tote bag. "I think I left my portable cell charger in your room. Can I go check?"

"Sure. Want me to come?" He wiggled his eyebrows.

She hit his arm. "You have to meet Jack and I have a feeling that you have no interest in getting my charger."

"Sure I do. But as long as we're up there…"

She hit him again. "Down, boy." She pocketed the key he handed over.

His face had been relaxed as they'd bantered back and forth. But suddenly, a line formed on his forehead and his eyes darkened. "Listen, Grace, when you get back, I'd like to talk to you about something."

She clamped down on the worry that crept up her spine. "Is everything okay?" she asked.

He framed her face with his hands and kissed her slowly and thoroughly. "Things are very okay."

She would have to accept that for now. With a last look, she turned and walked away.

Grace made her way to Xander's room and let herself in. She saw her charger immediately. After she threw it in her bag, she turned and Xander's key flew out of her hand. She bent to retrieve it, but as she straightened, something on the coffee table caught her eye.

It looked like Xander had been doing some work this afternoon. Next to a small portable printer, an official-looking document was lying on the table for anyone to peruse. She bit her lip. She didn't want housekeeping, or anyone else, to go through someone's personal files so she lifted her hand to flip it over. But at the sight of Emerson's name, she froze.

Grace knew she shouldn't have, but she couldn't help it. Her eyes were faster than her brain and they scanned the document.

It was a prenuptial agreement. For Emerson and Jack. Made by Xander. She frowned. She didn't realize Em and Jack had a prenup.

*None of your business.*

Still, she couldn't keep the disappointment at bay. Anyone who saw the two of them together would have no doubt they would be together forever.

Then she spotted something else. The document had today's date.

She scrunched up her nose. Today? That meant Xander had put this together...today?

A sickening feeling washed over her and she felt like a hundred-pound weight was falling in her stomach. Her gaze flicked back to the bed, where they'd loved each other all night. All of Xander's sweet words and tender gestures came flooding back to her.

Maybe none of it meant anything to him. How could it when he'd left their bed only to put together a prenup for Jack and Emerson?

She placed a hand to her heart, desperately trying to calm its rapid beating. Her other hand went to her mouth, holding in the cry that wanted to escape.

*How could he?*

All of her fairy-tale dreams came crashing down around

her. Pumpkin smashed, glass slippers shattered, twinkling stars dimmed.

This wasn't how it was supposed to go.

Out of all the many variations of dream relationships she'd had, never once did a prenup show up. Love was love. It was concrete and resolute, unwavering in its veracity.

Hadn't Xander complimented Em and Jack's relationship just last night? Then he'd romanced her all night. The things he said…the way he looked at her. What was all of that? She'd made it clear that she would sleep with him. There was no need for the facade of romance.

She gripped the prenup so hard that she actually wrinkled it. These papers represented the opposite of everything she believed in.

Love. Dedication. Devotion. Happily-ever-after.

And she thought…well, maybe she assumed, that Xander had come around to feel the same way. At least, that's what she wished. But it wasn't coming true.

Her heart hurt. But she didn't want to think about that. She wanted to focus everything in her being on her anger. That was easier. Except she couldn't. Because sadness was much stronger than anger.

She gingerly placed the document on the table the way one might handle a live bomb. Quietly, she left the room, determined to find Xander and figure out what exactly was going on. Did he believe in love and romance, or was he so scarred that he would never allow his walls to fall?

Sadly, she thought she already knew the answer. And it broke her heart.

## *Chapter Sixteen*

Xander was still laughing at Jack's feeble attempts to get the content of his best-man speech out of him. Eventually, Emerson had appeared and rolled her eyes at the pair of them. Then she dragged away a protesting Jack. One more reason to love Emerson Dewitt.

The lobby was a flurry of activity. Xander sat back in a plush chair, content to people-watch as the wedding guests arrived. He knew some of them, of course, and offered his hellos.

The earlier sun had been replaced with clouds. The sound of thunder could be heard in the distance as the first drops of rain began to fall outside.

He overheard Emerson's mother telling her that rain was good luck for a wedding. Xander had heard that saying before, but he always wondered if it was true or just something people said to appease anxious brides. In any case, he sat back and watched the lightning show outside the large windows.

Just as another bolt lit up the sky and thunder crackled right overhead, Grace appeared in the lobby. His body reacted immediately at the sight of her. He could feel his lips turn up into what was surely a goofy grin.

But something wasn't right. His smile faded as quickly as it had come. The ease and grace that usually surrounded her was absent. Tension engulfed her body. He could tell by the rigidity of her shoulders. Her eyes trained on him and her hands curled into fists.

She walked in a short, fast clip until she was right in front of him. Closer now, he could see that her emerald eyes were a much darker shade of green as they laser-focused on his face. Her cheeks were tinged with red.

What had happened? He hoped she wasn't upset about the weather. Although, with the way she was throwing death stares at him, he couldn't pretend this mood had to do with the wedding.

"What's wrong?" he asked.

Her lips trembled. "How could you?" There may have been anger in her eyes, but her words were dripping in sadness.

The lobby was packed. Xander noticed quite a few heads turn in their direction. He attempted to usher her to a different, quieter, part of the room, but quickly realized that was a mistake. She shook off his hands and stepped back. Her voice rushed out on a shaky breath.

"I saw the prenup in your room."

*Huh?* It took him a second to comprehend what she was saying. "Oh, the prenup for Jack and Emerson?"

She looked at him as if he'd just said something ridiculous. "Ah, yes. That prenup."

He wasn't getting it. "What's the problem with a prenup?"

"What's the problem?" She blew out a breath of exasperation. "Just last night you claimed Emerson and Jack were an amazing couple. Today, you make them a prenup."

"What does one thing have to do with another?"

"Did Jack or Em ask you to make that up for them?" she asked, biting her lip.

"Ah, no. I did it as a sort of gift for them."

She slapped a hand to his chest. "You either believe in love or you don't."

He stepped back. She was being completely irrational

and the audience around them was growing by the second. "Grace, can we go somewhere and talk about this like two rational adults?"

She reared back, even more color tinting her face. "No, we can stay right here. And I'm not the one being irrational. How dare you doubt Em and Jack's love."

"I'm not doubting anything," he said quietly. His patience was running thin. He glanced around the room, attempting to offer a small smile and convey that everything was fine. "Grace, can we please step outside?" His stomach was starting to twist into knots. He really hated public scenes, especially when they were negative.

"No," she said, determination in the small word even as her eyes widened and moisture threatened to spill over. "Answer my question."

"Fine. The bigger question is how can you get this mad over a document that has nothing to do with you? That prenup was about Jack and Emerson."

"What? How can you…?" She tugged on a strand of her hair, suddenly seeming very young and very naive. "You believe in prenups."

"I'm a divorce attorney. Of course I do. It's a very easy way to protect yourself and your assets."

"Prenups aren't… I mean, you can't… Love is… You're wrong."

She sounded like a child, and that's what it took for Xander's anger to dissipate. A realization hit him faster than the lightning outside. Despite her resolve, it wasn't anger that was emanating from Grace. When he looked deep into her eyes, he saw fear.

Grace Harris was afraid to let someone love her.

He remembered the story about her mother. The selfish woman who hadn't put her child first. How did someone get over that? She had to carry that with her on a daily basis.

His heart ached for her. She'd grown up with a mother who didn't care. Even though her grandparents had swooped in and rescued her, there had to be permanent scars.

This was heavy stuff. How could someone who'd begun her life without love, learn to love now? For Grace, she'd buried herself in fairy tales and storybook romances. That was fine for the average child, but for someone who had no other basis of real love, that had to mess with her perception

"You are *not* the man I thought you were," she said on a shaky breath.

A quick glance around the room showed him that they were definitely the main attraction. Everyone, including the hotel employees, was watching their show.

His first instinct was to run. This whole situation— Grace's outburst —was a little too reminiscent of his parents. All of those holidays and big parties when his parents had fought and made scenes and embarrassed him.

Emerson and Jack came around the corner hand in hand. They stopped, trying to assess the situation. They wore twin expressions of concern.

At the sight of his best friend, Jack's earlier words came back to Xander. His parents' relationship had no bearing on him and his relationship with Grace. He should fight back. He should shut down. Instead, he did something completely unexpected.

"I'm in love with you, Grace."

The statement took the wind out of her sails. He knew the feeling. He couldn't believe what he'd just said. He waited for the regret to set in, or even embarrassment. It didn't. In fact, he felt relieved. Happy that he'd been able to speak his truth. Shocked that he'd been able to express an emotion that he'd always assumed would evade him.

Grace's mouth dropped open. Her shoulders collapsed and all of the fight appeared to go out of her.

"That's right," he said quietly. "I'm in love with you. I love you." He blocked out all the pairs of eyes trained on them. At this moment, it was only about the two of them.

He knew she wouldn't return his sentiment. Not right now. But he also knew it was important that she hear it.

"You—you, uh, you don't know what you're saying," she said, her words tumbling over each other. She pointed at him. "You're just trying to distract me from the real issue."

"The real issue is that you're scared," he said calmly.

She shook her head, almost violently. "The real issue is that you aren't right for me." She waved a hand between them. "This isn't right. This isn't the way it's supposed to be. You can't say you love me and not believe in love at the same time."

"I believe in what I feel for you, and I know that's love."

"I can't do this with you." She took a step backward, and then another. With a last glare at him, she turned on her heel and fled toward the hallway.

"Grace," he called after her.

She didn't turn around, didn't face him. But she did pause and glance over her shoulder. He'd take it.

"I still love you," he said resolutely.

A mixture of emotions passed over her face. Then, she shook her head and walked away from him.

Xander didn't know what would happen. But the one thing he was sure of was that he'd spoken his truth. The curse his parents had started had been broken. Now he was living and now he could truly love.

The only question was whether Grace would be brave enough to love him back.

He loved her?

How dare Xander utter those three precious words—the most coveted words—to her as she attempted to call him out on that prenup. That wasn't how it was supposed to go. Professing love was a once-in-a-lifetime experience. It should be magical and romantic. Not hastily said during a heated moment.

Did he even mean it? Did Xander really...love her?

She took a deep breath, but it did little to calm her frayed nerves.

Did she love him?

"Doesn't matter," she said out loud to no one in particular, except the empty hallway. And it didn't matter. Because Xander wasn't the man she thought he was. Their relationship wasn't following the correct path.

Her heart ached again. She stopped walking and actually pressed a hand to her chest. Confused and torrid emotions swirled around her. How was she supposed to react to this?

Emerson came flying down the hallway. "What was all that about?" she asked. Her friend was practically running to catch up with her. She felt Emerson's hand on her arm. She paused and then slowly turned to face her. Meeting Em's concerned gaze, tears stung her eyes. Attempting to steady herself, she meant to take a long, calming breath.

"He's not the man for me," she said, her chest tightening.

"But, I see the way you guys look at each other."

"Well, forget about that," Grace said. She threw her arms out for extra measure.

"What happened?" Emerson asked.

"It's complicated."

Emerson studied her for a long time. Finally, she linked fingers with Grace. "Come on. Let's go to my room."

They made their way to Emerson's suite on the third floor, where flowers had been delivered. The sweet scents of roses and peonies filled the room. Her wedding gown hung on the door of the closet. Grace walked to it and ran her fingers over the elaborate beading.

Seeing the dress only made the tears come again.

"Gracie, sit."

Emerson was on the couch. She patted the cushion next to her. Grace went to her and they clasped hands.

"Tell me everything."

Grace told her about what had happened between her and Xander since coming to the hotel. How they'd become intimate, and how she'd thought he was changing his stance on relationships.

"That's wonderful, Gracie."

"I thought so, too. But I was wrong." Her lip began to tremble. "You need to know something, Em."

Emerson looked up.

Grace needed to warn her friend, but she truly didn't want to be the one to cause her pain. Surely this news would upset Emerson deeply.

Grace took a deep breath. "Xander is going to give you a prenup." She held her breath.

Emerson scrunched up her nose. "A what?"

"A prenuptial agreement. It's a contract that—"

Emerson covered Grace's hand with her own. "I know what a prenup is, Gracie, and Jack and I are not getting one."

"Em, I saw it." She told her about finding the document in Xander's room.

"Gracie, you're wrong. Jack and I already talked about a prenup."

"You did?"

"Yeah. I brought it up. My parents' pastor gave us a list of difficult things to discuss before our wedding. You know about those lists. Hard topics that aren't easy to talk about, but really should be discussed."

Grace nodded.

"So we went through the list. It had everything on it from children to where you want to live to when you want to retire.

And it had a ton of stuff about finances, including prenups. So I brought it up to Jack, but he didn't want one."

"He didn't?"

Emerson nodded.

"But—but… I saw the document and your names were on it. So was Xander's," she said in a low voice. "He made it for you. Today." She rose suddenly, needing to pace.

Emerson scratched her head. "I don't get it. What's the big deal if Xander did offer us a prenup?"

"It's not about the prenup. It's about…well, it's about love and believing in love."

"Please sit down, Gracie. You're not making any sense."

"I believe in love and marriage and happily-ever-afters."

"And sometimes that's a beautiful thing," Emerson said.

"Right—"

Emerson cut her off. "But not always. It isn't practical, Grace. You can't run around thinking you're in a romantic comedy."

"But that's what I want," she said in a soft, strangled voice. A lump formed in her throat.

All she'd ever wanted was to be part of a fairy tale. Ever since she'd been taken away from her mother—maybe even before then—she'd wished and hoped that everything would magically come together for her. That she would get to live out her princess fantasy. And it would be perfect.

"I don't mean to be so hard on you, Gracie. I just don't want you to miss out on something wonderful that's right in front of you because you're too busy waiting for some unrealistic prince to come along."

"I don't understand."

Emerson's eyes filled with understanding. "You always give men at least three chances. Even if the first date was horrible, you always give them the benefit of the doubt."

"I do."

"I always respected that about you. But then I started to notice something. After the third date, you seemed to come up with some reason why that man wasn't perfect. Don't get me wrong, sometimes I agreed with you. Remember the guy with the dummy?"

Grace actually laughed. "Please don't remind me. And let's not forget Derek."

Emerson groaned. "I can't even." Her eyebrows drew down in concentration and she leaned in. "But I started noticing that you were finding more and more reasons as to why a guy wasn't the one for you."

"Em—"

"I think you're afraid to be loved."

That's what Xander had said to her.

Grace tried to pull away, but Emerson held on to her hand. She squeezed it tightly, showing Grace that she was there for her.

It was true. Emerson's words were hard to hear, but they were spot on. She didn't have to think long and hard as to the why. It was because of her mother.

"You're never going to get a perfect life, Gracie. Perfect doesn't exist. And why would you want one?"

When she put it like that… Grace felt overwhelmed. Was she really afraid of love? Did she fear the one emotion she valued more than any other? In her experience, love brought pain and hurt. Her mother's face flashed before her eyes.

Emerson lightly tapped Grace's temple. "You can stay in here, waiting and hoping and wishing for your Prince Charming. Or you can open your eyes and see that he may just be right in front of you and answering to the name of Xander Ryan."

Grace had been thinking of her mother, but her thoughts turned to her grandparents—two people who'd dropped everything in their lives to rescue her. They raised her with love and kindness.

She thought about Emerson, her best friend, and the person who had been there for her every single day since they'd met. They weren't technically sisters, yet Emerson filled that role.

"As for this prenup business, I don't know what Xander was thinking," Emerson said. "But I'm sure he has some reasonable explanation. Believe it or not, Xander actually helped Jack realize his feelings for me."

"Really?"

Emerson nodded. "Oh, yeah."

Grace's phone began ringing. "It's Grammy."

Emerson rose. "Stay as long as you want. I'm going to let Jack know you're okay. You are okay, right?"

Grace nodded slowly. "I will be. Thanks, Em."

"Anytime."

As Emerson left her suite, Grace answered her Grammy's call. Hearing her sweet voice was exactly what she needed at the moment. She couldn't wait for tomorrow, when her grandparents would be in Virginia for the wedding. Seeing them in person and being able to wrap her arms around them would surely fix everything.

They talked about her grandparents' flight and details for the hotel. But Grammy paused. Grace always thought her grandmother was psychic. How did she always know when something was wrong?

"Is everything okay, sweetie pie?" she asked.

"Of course. Just busy getting everything ready for tomorrow." She bit her lip. She never liked lying to Grammy.

"Hmm, I know this wedding came up on you fast, and I'm sure you've spent your fair share of sleepless nights. But why don't you tell me what's really happening."

Grace sighed. Then she did as Grammy instructed. She

spilled the whole thing. From when she'd first met Xander until today and finding that prenup.

"I thought he was changing. But obviously he doesn't really believe in love."

"Didn't that boy just tell you that he loved you?"

"Well, yes, but…"

Grammy tsked. "No *but* about it. If a man who struggles with love and relationships tells a woman who is in the process of yelling at him that he loves her, trust me, sweetie, he means it."

Grace crumpled down to the sofa. "Well, I don't want a relationship like this. It's not the way it's supposed to be."

"Love comes in all different shapes and sizes. There's no perfect mold. Look at us."

*Huh?* "What do you mean?" Grace asked.

"I'm your grandmother, but I love you as if you were my own child."

Grace's eyes filled. "Oh, Grammy."

"Maybe I read you too many fairy tales when you were little."

The idea was shocking.

Grammy continued. "The point is not to copy a fairy tale that's already been written. Real life and real love are all about writing your own story. From start to finish."

Finally, Grace didn't attempt to hold the tears back. They ran down her face as she sniffled into the phone.

"It sounds like this Xander really does love you. And why wouldn't he?"

"He said he did," she said in a hushed voice. "Even after I stormed off. He said he still loved me."

"Then I can't wait to meet him tomorrow. We already have one thing in common."

"What's that?"

"We both know how stubborn you are." She chuckled,

then paused. When she spoke again, her voice had taken on the soft, patient tone Grace always associated with her Grammy. "And yet we love you just as you are. Don't let real love get away from you, sweetheart. Go grab it and hold it close."

After they hung up, Grace closed her eyes and tried to absorb everything that had happened today. But all she could think of was Xander and her Grammy's wise words. *Don't let real love get away from you.*

A smile blossomed on her face. She was in love with Xander. She was in love with someone whom she fought with constantly. She was in love with a divorce attorney. She was in love with a wonderful man who loved her back.

She left Emerson's suite with a new determination, and began walking down the hallway. She took the elevator down to the first floor.

Amelia, Emerson's sister, called Grace's name as she made her way toward the lobby. "Hey, Grace, I'm supposed to check on the flowers for tomorrow. Do you know what time they are expected to arrive? Also, my mom texted and said the photographer showed up early."

Grace stared at her. She knew Amelia was saying something, something that was probably important that pertained to the wedding. But all she cared about in this moment was Xander. She had to find him.

"Uh, Grace? You okay?"

Grace giggled. "I've never been better. I'm in love with Xander Ryan!"

Amelia's mouth opened and closed and then she blew a breath out, fanning her hair around her face. "O-kay. So-o-o, where should we put the photographer?"

Again, Grace laughed. "I don't know. I mean, I do. I will. I need to add something to my very long list of things to do.

I need to go tell the man I love that I'm sorry. Then, I'll get back to our regularly scheduled program."

Mrs. Dewitt came bustling down the hallway. "Amelia, did you tell Grace about the photographer?"

Amelia gave Grace a long once-over. Finally, she grinned as she turned to her mom. "I did. But Grace has something really important to take care of first. Go," she whispered, urging Grace along.

With a laugh trailing after her, Grace ran into the lobby. She scanned all of the people milling about but didn't see Xander. She frowned and turned in a circle. She ran back down the hall and checked the restaurant. He wasn't there, either.

She pulled out her phone to call him but saw that it had turned off. She'd never charged it after getting her charger from Xander's room.

"Shoot," she said to herself.

She ran up to his room and banged on the door. No answer. She didn't think he was the type to ignore her so she returned to the lobby. Just as she was about to give up, she spotted someone through the large windows.

Xander was standing under the far side of the portico staring off at the falling rain. She rushed past wedding guests and hotel staff, barely avoiding a crash with a luggage cart.

The air had turned chilly, as the rain had cooled everything off. The wind was whipping through the trees and she could still hear thunder off in the distance.

As she approached him, she could see that Xander was deep in thought. He was staring straight ahead, his hands buried in his pockets. He was already wearing the suit for tonight's dinner. Once again, she was struck by how handsome he was.

She stood silently, about three feet from him. He must have sensed her because he turned, his eyes meeting hers.

"Grace," he said.

"Xander." Suddenly, she was nervous. Her earlier confidence had evaporated. She wiped her damp palms on her pants. "Hi."

"Hi," he said, mimicking her. He wasn't going to make this easy on her. She deserved that.

Tentatively, she stepped toward him. "Xander, I'm sorry. I talked to Em and then I spoke with my grammy, and I realized that I overreacted, and that, well, I had some issues to work through."

He stared at her for a long moment, not saying anything. She gulped. Maybe she'd really messed this up. Maybe he wouldn't forgive her. Maybe he didn't want to hear anything from her.

But then, just as a large gust of wind blew the rain in their direction, Xander's face lit up with a huge grin. As raindrops dotted his face, he closed the gap between them.

"Did you say you were sorry?"

She wiped water from her cheeks. "I did. And I am. Sorry, I mean. It's just that with my mother and then because of—"

She didn't have a chance to finish that sentence because his lips were on hers. It was as if everything had clicked into place. She wound her arms around his neck as his came around her waist, pulling her closer as the wind continued to push the rain onto them.

When their lips finally parted, she looked up at him and smiled. "I am sorry, Xander. I was scared."

He nodded, as if he already knew this. "I didn't mean to scare you."

"It wasn't you. It was me. All me."

He kissed her forehead, still holding on to her tightly. "Does this mean you aren't angry with me anymore?"

She shook her head. "Not at all. Although, I'm sure you'll do something to tick me off shortly."

He chuckled. "I'll try. In the meantime, I want to repeat something. I love you, Grace Harris."

They were soaked to the bone and the rain continued to fall. In a movie or a storybook, this is where the rain would magically stop and a rainbow would replace it. The music would swell as she returned his sentiment.

But this wasn't a movie or a storybook. This was real. And it was hers. Her moment.

And Grace was determined to grab hold and take it.

She pushed her wet hair out of her eyes. "I love you, too, Xander Ryan."

His mouth was on hers again until she gently pushed him back. "We don't have to get engaged or married. The only thing I want from you is love."

"Well, you got that. In spades."

She grinned and kissed him again. The rain continued to fall. In fact, it didn't stop all night. No rainbows appeared, or magical crickets sang.

Yet, it was the best ending she'd ever experienced in her life.

# *Epilogue*

"Merry Christmas, sleepyhead."

Grace rolled over to find her favorite sight in the world: Xander's big grin. Lazily, she ran a hand up his arm, disappointed that he was wearing pajamas.

"Merry Christmas to you." Her voice was gruff from a restful night's sleep in her childhood bed in Orlando.

They were spending the week of Christmas with her grandparents. So far everything was going better than expected. Grammy and Pops adored Xander. Grammy confided that she thought Xander was "one hot babe" and Pops seemed to be enjoying peppering Xander with legal questions.

They'd been busy, too. They'd visited several of the local theme parks, done some last-minute Christmas shopping, and even made cookies with Grammy. The highlight for Grace was the night Grammy and Pops' housing development shot off fireworks. Xander wrapped his arms around her and whispered how much he loved her. Then he'd presented her with the most beautiful and thoughtful gift she'd ever received. He'd held a bubblegum-pink box that had clearly been meant for a little girl. When he cracked it open, she saw the children's princess ring she'd wanted as a child.

He slipped it on her ring finger as the last firework hit the sky.

"You are my princess. Always."

She'd been too moved to say anything. Instead, she'd kissed him with as much passion as she could muster.

Grace began to sit up in bed when the welcoming aroma of coffee caught her attention. "You brought me coffee." Then she shot up. "Wait, if Pops finds you in here, you're a dead man. Not even Santa will be able to help you." Her grandparents approved of Xander, but they were old-school in their beliefs. No sharing bedrooms.

He chuckled. The warm tone of his laughter soothed her the way it did every time she heard it.

"Don't worry. Your grandparents went for an early morning walk."

Grace glanced at the clock on the bedside table. It read seven thirty. "How long have you guys been up?"

"Since five," Xander said with a grin. "I played a round of gin with Pops. Then Grammy woke up and made me coffee and cinnamon toast. Have I mentioned that I could live here forever?"

She giggled. "I know the feeling. I'm just happy that you all love each other."

"What's not to love? Your grandparents are amazing. They feed me, they spoil you, this house is the best."

Grace reached for the mug of coffee and relished the first sip. Xander knew exactly how she liked it.

He took his own mug and joined her in bed, placing the tray he'd carried in between them. That's when she noticed two wrapped presents on it.

The sight of presents always made Grace resort to her seven-year-old self. She gasped in delight. "Xander, what are these? I've already seen the presents you put under the tree for me."

He rubbed the back of his neck. For once, her superconfident boyfriend seemed a little less sure of himself. Curiosity rose within her.

He gestured to the two presents. "These are kind of special. I really hope you like them."

"I'm sure I'll love them." She couldn't imagine what had him acting so anxious.

Xander held up one of the boxes. "Open this first."

She took the offered present and ripped open the paper.

"No dainty tearing of the paper for you, I see." He laughed.

"This princess likes to get right to the point."

She threw the Santa-themed wrapping paper to the floor and turned the box over in her hand. When it dawned on her what she was looking at, she glanced up to meet his eyes.

"It's one of those DNA testing kits from Ancestry.com." He ran a hand through his hair, messing up his already morning-mussed hairstyle. "I hope this isn't too presumptuous. It's just that I know you feel lost not knowing your father's side of your family tree." He tapped the box. "This won't introduce you to your dad, but it might help answer some of your questions." He coughed. "Or, you know, just bring you some clarity."

He was still nervous and Grace thought it was adorable. She turned the box over and quickly read the description.

Why hadn't she thought of this herself? She could take a DNA test and find out where she was from. Xander was right. It wouldn't introduce her to her father but it would bring her closer to that side of her family. Closer than ever before.

"Listen, Grace, I hope you're not upset—"

She put a finger to his lips and then replaced it with her lips. When she pulled away, she smiled. "Thank you." And she kissed him again.

"I guess this means you like it."

"I love it. Thank you, thank you, thank you. This is probably the most thoughtful gift anyone's ever given me."

"Well, damn. That doesn't bode well for this next present."

She leaned forward, raising her eyebrows in question.

Xander held the present out for her. It was wrapped in metallic silver paper with a huge red bow on top.

This time, she didn't rip right into the present. Something had her slowly unwrapping it. Once the paper was gone, she opened the box lid and laughed. There was another wrapped present inside.

"Xander," she said.

"If you can't have fun at Christmas, I don't know when you can."

She opened the next present, wrapped in red paper with bright green Christmas trees. When she lifted the lid of that box, there was yet another present.

Laughing, Grace went through three more rounds until she was left with a small pink jewelry box.

"Isn't this…?"

Xander nodded. "The same box as your pretty, pretty princess ring? I recycled it," he said proudly.

"You're so weird."

She lifted the lid expecting to find another princess ring. Or maybe a pair of mouse earrings or a princess pin. What she saw made her gasp so hard that she actually dropped the box in her lap.

Xander grabbed it and held it up to her again.

With shaking hands, she took the box and peered inside. A large princess-cut diamond surrounded by smaller but no less sparkly diamonds, set on a delicate platinum band stared back at her.

She hadn't realized Xander had moved. But when he spoke, she saw that he was at the side of the bed, down on one knee. He reached for one of her hands.

"Princess Grace, I love you more than I ever thought one person could love another. I want to spend the rest of my life being your Prince Charming."

# AVAILABLE THIS MONTH FROM
## Harlequin® Special Edition

### FORTUNE'S FRESH START
*The Fortunes of Texas: Rambling Rose* • by Michelle Major

In the small Texas burg of Rambling Rose, real estate investor Callum Fortune is making a big splash. The last thing he needs is any personal complications slowing his pace—least of all nurse Becky Averill, a beautiful widow with twin baby girls!

### HER RIGHT-HAND COWBOY
*Forever, Texas* • by Marie Ferrarella

A clause in her father's will requires Ena O'Rourke to work the family ranch for six months before she can sell it. She's livid at her father throwing a wrench in her life from beyond the grave. But Mitch Randall, foreman of the Double E, is always there for her. As Ena spends more time on the ranch—and with Mitch—new memories are laid over the old...and perhaps new opportunities to make a life.

### SECOND-CHANCE SWEET SHOP
*Wickham Falls Weddings* • by Rochelle Alers

Brand-new bakery owner Sasha Manning didn't anticipate that the teenager she hired would have a father more delectable than anything in her shop window! Sasha still smarts from falling for a man too good to be true. Divorced single dad Dwight Adams will have to prove to Sasha that he's the real deal and not a wolf in sheep's clothing...and learn to trust someone with his heart along the way.

### COOKING UP ROMANCE
*The Taylor Triplets* • by Lynne Marshall

Lacy was a redhead with a pink food truck who prepared mouthwatering meals. Hunky construction manager Zack Gardner agreed to let her feed his hungry crew in exchange for cooking lessons for his young daughter. But it looked like the lovely businesswoman was transforming the single dad's life in more ways than one—since a family secret is going to change both of their lives in ways they never expected.

### RELUCTANT HOMETOWN HERO
*Wildfire Ridge* • by Heatherly Bell

Former army officer Ryan Davis doesn't relish the high-profile role of town sheriff, but when duty calls, he responds. Even if it means helping animal rescuer Zoey Castillo find her missing foster dog. When Ryan asks her out, Zoey is wary of a relationship in the spotlight—especially given her past. If the sheriff wants to date her, he'll have to prove that two legs are better than four.

### THE WEDDING TRUCE
*Something True* • by Kerri Carpenter

For the sake of their best friends' wedding, divorce attorney Xander Ryan and wedding planner Grace Harris are calling a truce. Now they must plan the perfect wedding shower together. But Xander doesn't believe in marriage! And Grace believes in romance and true love. Clearly, they have nothing in common. In fact, all Xander feels when Grace is near is disdain and...desire. Wait. What?

**LOOK FOR THESE AND OTHER HARLEQUIN SPECIAL EDITION BOOKS WHEREVER BOOKS ARE SOLD, INCLUDING MOST BOOKSTORES, SUPERMARKETS, DISCOUNT STORES AND DRUGSTORES.**

HSEATMBPA0120

# YOU HAVE JUST READ A HARLEQUIN® SPECIAL EDITION BOOK.

Discover more heartfelt tales of **family, friendship** and **love** from the Harlequin Special Edition series. Be sure to look for all six Harlequin® Special Edition books every month.

HARLEQUIN®
## SPECIAL EDITION

*We've got some exciting changes coming in our
February 2020 Special Edition books!
Our covers have been redesigned, and the emotional
contemporary romances from your favorite authors
will be longer in length.*

*Be sure to come back next month for more great stories
from Special Edition!*

*Look for Amelia's story,
the next book in Kerri Carpenter's
Something True miniseries for
Harlequin Special Edition.
Coming soon, wherever Harlequin books
and ebooks are sold!*

Her voice came out as barely a whisper. "But I thought you didn't believe in marriage."

His eyes were more serious than she'd ever seen before. "With you, I believe in everything. Marry me, Grace Harris."

She was off the bed and into his arms faster than Rudolph could fly. As she pressed her lips to his, she muttered her answer. "Yes."

They spent the rest of the day celebrating. Her grandparents were thrilled and couldn't stop hugging both her and Xander. They had champagne for breakfast and Christmas cookies for lunch. In other words, it was the most perfect day ever.

As day faded into night and the Christmas lights were turned on, Grace looked down at her new engagement ring. She couldn't believe where she'd ended up.

When she thought about how her life had started back in West Virginia and how scared and lonely she'd been as a child, it was miraculous she'd become the person she was. A few months ago, she'd still been reaching for something to help her feel complete. Yet, she needn't have worried.

Grace Harris was finally getting the happily-ever-after of her dreams.

\* \* \* \* \*